WE SO SELDOM

LOOK ON LOVE

ALSO BY BARBARA GOWDY

Through the Green Valley

Fallen Angels

Mister Sandman

The White Bone

The Romantic

Helpless

WE SO SELDOM
LOOK ON LOVE

BARBARA GOWDY

ZOLAND BOOKS

AN IMPRINT OF STEERFORTH PRESS
HANOVER, NEW HAMPSHIRE

For information about permission to reproduce selections
from this book, write to: Steerforth Press L.L.C.,
45 Lyme Road, Suite 208,
Hanover, New Hampshire 03755

This book was originally published in Toronto, Ontario
in 1992 by Somerville House Publishing and in the United States by
HarperCollins Publishers.

"Ode on Necrophilia" from *The Collected Poems of Frank O'Hara,* copyright
© 1971 by Maureen Granville-Smith, Administratrix of the Estate of Frank
O'Hara, reprinted by permission of Alfred A. Knopf, Inc.

The Library of Congress Cataloging-in-Publication Data
Gowdy, Barbara.
We so seldom look on love / Barbara Gowdy. — 1st pbk. ed.
p.   cm.
ISBN 1-883642-00-0 (alk. paper)
1. Body. Human—Fiction.   I. Title.
PR9199.3.G658W4   1997
813'.54—dc21   97-2887
CIP

ISBN 13: 978-1-883642-00-6

Manufactured in the United States of America

Well,
    it is better
            that
                O M E O N
            S   love them   E
and we
    so seldom look on love
                    that it seems heinous

            – *"Ode on Necrophilia,"* Frank O'Hara

To my sister, Beth

Certain of these stories, in somewhat different form, have been previously published:

"Body and Soul" in *Descant*, Number 75, Volume 22, Number 4

"Sylvie" in *Story*, Spring 1992

"Ninety-three Million Miles Away," in *Canadian Fiction Magazine*, Twentieth Anniversary Issue, Number 74/5, winner of *Canadian Fiction Magazine*'s Annual Contributor's Prize. Also in *Slow Hand—Women Writing Erotica*, edited by Michele Slung, Harper Collins, New York, 1992

"The Two-Headed Man" in *Quarry*, Volume 39, Number 4

"We So Seldom Look on Love," in *Canadian Fiction Magazine*, Number 73.

The author is grateful for the support of the Toronto Arts Council, the Ontario Arts Council and the Canada Council.

CONTENTS

BODY AND SOUL

for Annie Dillard and Marius von Senden

IN THE APARTMENT BUILDING across from theirs, six storeys above the ground, a cat walks along a balcony railing.

"Cat," Julie announces, then stretches open her mouth in a pantomime of her mother screaming when there was a cat in their toilet.

"What colour is it?" Terry asks.

"Black and white."

"Oh, black and *white*." Terry's disdain is her second foster mother's disdain for black-and-white movies.

"Black and white and black and white and black and white," Julie shouts, hitting her doll on the window-ledge.

"I heard you," Terry says primly. As she turns from the window there is a sound from outside like a siren starting up. She is about to ask what was that? but instead she screams, "Aunt Bea!" because Julie has begun to make the sink-draining noise in her throat. "Aunt Bea!"

"I'm coming," Aunt Bea says, her sandals clicking into the room. Terry is bumped aside by her big hip, while Julie, who isn't having an epileptic seizure, pushes away Aunt Bea's arm.

"Now," Aunt Bea chides, but Julie slaps the pencil out of Aunt Bea's hand, then abruptly shuts up, providing a moment of dreamlike silence that signals to Aunt Bea the presence of the Lord. She feels her blood pressure draining from her temples like mercury down a thermometer. She smiles into Julie's pearl-coloured eyes and says, "I guess we had a false alarm."

Julie's features contort into an expression of ugly, inconsolable, private and measureless grief.

"You're all right now?" Aunt Bea says. She can never be sure, but she assumes that Julie is smiling back at her.

"Penny—" Julie points her doll at the window.

"Yes?" Terry says. "Penny" is what Julie calls Terry, nobody knows why.

Julie forgets what she was going to say. She begins hitting her doll on the window-pane.

"Hold your horses, I'm looking," Aunt Bea says, inserting her hand between Julie's doll and the window. She clutches the knob of the doll's head. "Good heavens," she says.

"What?" Terry cries.

Aunt Bea dips her chin to see out the top of her bifocals. "Well," she says, "there seems to be a cat lying out there in the parking lot."

"Fell," Julie says in an anguished voice.

"Oh, did it," Aunt Bea says. "Oh, dear."

"Dead," Julie says.

"No, no, I don't think so," Aunt Bea says, although

from the pool of blood and unnatural angle of the cat's head she's thinking, Dead as a doornail.

"Is it bleeding?" Terry cries.

Aunt Bea hears, "Is it *breathing?*" and her heart constricts. It never fails to constrict Aunt Bea's heart how eagle-eyed this little blind girl imagines everybody is. "Yes," she says slowly, as if she is scrutinizing, "yes, you know, I think its chest is moving up and down."

"Is it *bleeding?*" Terry repeats. She holds her hand out.

"It is *not* moving up and down," Julie says in a severely reproachful voice.

Aunt Bea would swear that the only time Julie speaks in complete sentences is to catch her in a lie. "It's hard to tell, of course," she says.

"But is it *bleeding?*" Terry cries. The faint emanation of heat that she senses in her extended hand is Aunt Bea's blood pressure going back up.

"Nobody seems to be coming down," Aunt Bea observes to change the subject.

"You better phone the Humane's Society," Terry cries.

"I guess so," Aunt Bea says. She snatches Terry's hand and squeezes it to calm the child. "All right, I'll go call them," she says, and leaves the room.

"Is it bleeding?" Terry asks Julie. Blood concerns Terry. Eyes, she was disturbed to learn, can bleed.

"Dead," Julie says.

"*But is it bleeding, I asked.*" Terry is on the verge of tears. She wants an answer to this question even though she never relies on what Julie says. Whenever Julie answers the phone and it's a woman, she always says, "It's my mother."

"Black and white and black and white," Julie says.

Terry sighs. "I know *that*," she says, giving up.

Julie, however, is referring to the checkered dress of a woman who has run across the parking lot and is now kneeling over the cat. Mommy! Julie thinks, ecstatic, and then she knows that it is not her mother, and she chews thoughtfully on her doll's foot.

"Bleeding doesn't mean you die, though," Terry says, making her way over to her dresser. With the palm of her hand she taps the bristles of her hairbrush for the tingling sensation that reminds her of drinking Coke. Julie believes that Coke *looks* bristly. Milk, being smooth, she thinks of as round. The only thing she cannot imagine, the only thing she is prepared to be surprised by, is colour.

Terry was born nine years ago to an eighteen-year-old migrant corn detassler who left the abortion too late, mostly out of curiosity as to who the father might be. By the colour of the baby's hair, she'd know. But Terry came into the world bald and blind and with a birthmark covering most of the left side of her face, and Terry's mother walked out of the hospital that same evening. To the nurse who tried to stop her, she hollered, "I coulda had her at home and thrown her in a dumpster, ya know!"

The nurses adored Terry. She hardly ever cried; in fact, she smiled most of the time. (Some of the nurses held this up as proof that a baby's smile indicated gas; others said it proved that smiling was innate and not learned.) During the day they kept her in a bassinet at their station, on a table next to the photocopier, where it was discovered that the rhythm of the cartridge moving back and forth sent her to sleep. When she was teething, the head nurse left written orders that the copier was to be kept going for as long as Terry fretted. The head nurse, a collector and exhibitor of ethnically dressed dolls, made outfits for Terry in her spare time. Crocheted gowns, elaborately frilled, embroidered and aproned dresses, matching bows backed with tape so they could be stuck to her bald head. The other nurses bought her toys and sleepers. If an adoption agency was coming by to take her picture, they dressed her up and dabbed make-up on her birthmark to give her a fighting chance.

No couples wanted her, though. It took two years for Children's Aid to come through with just a foster mother, and even *she* was obviously reluctant. Her name was Mrs. Stubbs. "Terry won't be getting any special treatment," she informed the nurses. "My own son's asthmatic, and I treat him exactly like my daughter." She refused to take the dresses because they had to be washed by hand and ironed. "I've got better things to do than that," she said.

Such as housecleaning. In Mrs. Stubbs's house the plastic was still on the lampshades, and Terry was taught to eat cookies with a hand cupped under her chin to catch the crumbs. There were two other children—the woman's daughter, who eloped when Terry was six, and the asthmatic son, who was devoted to goldfish. Once, he let Terry put her hand in the tank to feel fish swim by. She was startled by how soft and slimy they were; she had expected the cold hardness of her foster mother's wedding band. Her foster mother admired the glass-cleaning snails but was disgusted by the goldfish going to the bathroom in the very water that passed through their gills. The bathroom in her house smelled like pine cones. Terry was slapped for leaving the top off the toothpaste, for wearing her shoes in the house, for spilling anything—those were the worst offences. Living with this foster mother, she became a high-strung child with fingers like antennae. She could extend her hand and sense if another person was in the room. By the air currents passing through her fingers, she could tell if somebody was breathing in her direction.

Terry cried her heart out when she had to leave that home for a home closer to the school for the blind, but within a few days she loved her second foster mother to death. They spent most of their time together on the couch in front of the TV, one of the foster mother's arms around Terry, the other holding the channel changer, which she used every two minutes because she wouldn't watch commercials and because "Andy of Mayberry" was the only program that didn't drive her crazy.

"Oh, right, give us a break," she'd say to the newscaster, then eliminate him. "Christ," she'd say, tapping her long nails on the wooden armrest next to Terry, "who comes *up* with this shit?"

Terry squirmed at the bad language, but the "us" flattered and enthralled her.

Her second foster mother's husband was a jolly, long-distance truck driver. He came home once a week, then left early the next morning before Terry woke up. Terry's foster mother groaned at the sound of his rig pulling into the driveway. She made him pork and beans and sat smoking and sighing at the dinner table while he relayed with his mouth full the hilarious things that he and his buddies had said to each other over their short-wave radios. Terry rarely understood the joke, but she laughed because of his infectious laugh, and then he would mess her hair and say, "You liked that, eh, Orphan Annie?" When he stopped coming home at all, she wasn't surprised. If he'd been a man on their TV, he wouldn't have lasted five seconds.

But she *was* surprised—and so distressed she began pulling out her baby-fine hair in her sleep; nests of it in her clenched fist every morning—when she learned that his disappearance meant she would have to leave.

Her third foster mother lived two blocks away. In a voice very familiar to Terry she said, "Mrs. Brodie is too formal. I don't want you calling me that. How about if you just call me Aunt Joyce."

"How about if I call you Aunt Bea?" Terry said.

"Aunt Bea?" Mrs. Brodie's dead sister was named Bea, so she was taken aback.

"From 'Andy of Mayberry.'"

Mrs. Brodie smiled. "Well, you know, I have to admit there's a resemblance. She's got a bun, though, as I recall. And I've got glasses, which I don't think she has. Plus I'm about fifty pounds fatter. But our faces are kind of the same, you know, kind of . . ." She touched her face.

"Old," Terry offered. She took it for granted that everybody had the same face.

"Old!" Mrs. Brodie laughed. "That's right! Old! How would you like to help me bake a pie?"

The only bad thing about living with Aunt Bea was when her granddaughter, Marcy, came to visit. The first time she came she didn't speak until she and Terry were outside in the playground, and then she said, "Everybody hates you" and pinched Terry's arm.

Until then Terry had thought Marcy was a mute. There was a mute who used to play with her first foster mother's son. Despite the fact that Marcy's breath hit Terry at face level, Terry had pictured a soft, little mute you could hold in your hand. The pinch burst Marcy into the spiky shape of a scream. "Go home!" Terry cried.

"She's *my* grandmother!" Marcy shouted. "You're the one that better go home before I kill you!"

Terry began to run. But since she had a poor sense of direction and no concept of space, "far away" meaning simply that it took longer to get there than "nearby" did, she ran in a large circle and didn't realize until a split second before Marcy shrieked in her ear that she had ended up back where she started.

"They're getting along like a house on fire," Aunt Bea said.

She and her daughter, who was Marcy's mother, were keeping watch from the apartment. The daughter was trying to unlatch the window. She glanced over at Aunt Bea and thought, Jesus Christ, she's as deaf as a post. When she got the window open, she stuck her head out and yelled, "Marcy! Don't chase her out onto the road! Marcy! Do you hear me?"

"Yes!" Marcy hollered without looking up. She was racing to get a stick she had spotted in the sandbox. Terry stood very still and oblivious, like somebody waiting for a bus.

Sighing, Aunt Bea's daughter closed the window. She could hardly blame Marcy. Suddenly there was this stray living in her granny's apartment, sleeping in the bed that used to be reserved for *her*, playing with her Barbie doll. "I wish you'd talked this over with me first," she said.

"You don't have to shout," Aunt Bea said gently.

Marcy speared the stick straight at Terry, missing her by inches. "Oh, God," Aunt Bea's daughter said. She glanced at Aunt Bea's placid face. "They say you shouldn't make any big decisions for at least a year," she said. "Now you're tied down again."

Thank the Lord, Aunt Bea thought.

"Just don't get too attached to her," her daughter said. "She could be taken away at any time."

Aunt Bea crossed her arms over the ledge of her bosom and said, "Yesterday I made meringues, and when I gave her one, you know what she said?"

"I have no idea."

Aunt Bea chuckled. "She said, 'This is good styrofoam.'"

"I can't get it out of my mind that time I came

here and you'd left the burner on," her daughter said. "I'm going to worry myself sick when we're living in Saskatoon."

The idea was to get somebody full of beans like Marcy but a little older, eleven or twelve, maybe, somebody who could play with Terry and walk her to and from the school for the blind. That walk was the hardest part for Aunt Bea. The school wasn't far, just a couple of blocks, but in the mornings, until she'd been up and around for a while, her ankles were so swollen they hardly fit into her shoes.

Out of some mixup, however, the social worker brought over Julie. It was a weekday afternoon, and Terry was at school. At the social worker's recommendation Aunt Bea was waiting until she and the new girl— Esther, she had been told her name was—had met each other before she said anything to Terry. The visit was a trial. If Esther took a strong dislike to Aunt Bea (or vice versa, although Aunt Bea couldn't imagine disliking a child), then Children's Aid would come up with somebody else.

While she sat at the dining-room window keeping an eye out for the social worker's old blue Chevy, Aunt Bea busied herself with knitting a skating sweater that was gradually, in her mind, changing from Terry's to Esther's. When she saw the car, she quickly folded the knitting up and put it in the sideboard drawer, then turned to the window again. The social worker was striding around as if to open the passenger door, but it opened before she got there. Aunt Bea adjusted her bifocals to get a good look.

"Oh, my," she said out loud.

It was the name, Esther, that had misled her. She had pictured a Jewish girl—dark, undernourished . . . haunted Anne Frank eyes. She had pictured a cardigan sweater several sizes too small. The girl who climbed out of the car was fat—Lord, as fat as Aunt Bea herself—and she had short white-blond hair in some kind of crazy brushcut. She headed in a beeline for the wrong apartment building. When the social worker called her back, she turned on her heel and took up a new beeline. Like a remote-control car, Aunt Bea thought. There was something else funny about that walk, though . . . a looseness in the legs and torso, a struggle for co-ordination that didn't seem at all right.

"Poor thing," Aunt Bea said to herself. This was not so much sympathy as a resolute summoning of sympathy. "Poor little motherless thing."

She scarcely had the door open when the girl said, "Hi." She said it suddenly and loudly, as if to frighten Aunt Bea. Then she rolled her eyes as if she were about to black out.

"Hi! Come in! Come in!" Aunt Bea said enthusiastically, but she was thinking, "A retard," and now she really was thrown for a bit of a loop. "Don't sweat the petty things!" she said, reading the girl's sweatshirt.

"Believe me," the social worker said. "It was not my idea that she wear that." She took the girl's arm and turned her around.

"Pet the sweaty things," Aunt Bea read. She didn't get it.

"It belonged to her mother," the social worker said, giving Aunt Bea a confidential look.

"Oh?" Aunt Bea said.

"Come on, Julie, don't do that," the social worker said. The girl was bunching up the shirt with her fists, revealing a belly like a mound of virgin snow.

Julie? Aunt Bea thought.

"Should we take off our shoes?" the social worker asked.

"No, no," Aunt Bea said, blinking herself back into action. "Sit down anywhere. I've got shortbreads and chocolate milk, and coffee's made. Would you like some chocolate milk?" she asked. She looked at the girl and added, "Julie?"

"Coffee," Julie said loudly.

"Julie's been drinking coffee for years," the social worker said, falling into a chair. "*And* beer, *and* I shudder to thing what else." The social worker was a homely, frizzy-haired woman in dungarees and work boots. "Actually *I* wouldn't mind a glass of chocolate milk," she said.

Don't sweat the petty things, Aunt Bea said to herself as she poured the coffee. Pet the sweaty things. Speaking of sweat, her body was soaked in it. "Everything's fine," she told herself. "Everything's just fine and dandy." She hummed a hymn:

"A charge to keep I have,
A God to glorify,

A never-dying soul to save
And fit it for the sky."

The first thing she would do was give that crazy jail-
bird hair a perm.

Coming out of the kitchen, she asked Julie how old
she was. Fifteen was her guess.

"Five," Julie answered.

"Five?" Aunt Bea looked at the social worker.

"Eleven," the social worker said with mild exasperation.

Aunt Bea nodded. At least Children's Aid had got
that right. She handed Julie her coffee, and Julie immediately gulped half of it down.

"There isn't sugar in here," Julie said, holding up her
mug.

Aunt Bea was startled. She cast back to a moment
ago. "No, there's sugar."

"It's *not* sugar," Julie said. She looked infuriated.

"Oh!" Aunt Bea laughed. "Yes, you're right! It's
Sweet'n Low!" She beamed at the social worker. "I can't
tell the difference."

"Just drink it," the social worker said.

"No, no. I've got sugar." Aunt Bea hurried over to retrieve Julie's mug. She smiled into Julie's suddenly blank
eyes. Pale, pale pupils, almost white. Aunt Bea had never
seen eyes like that.

The social worker seemed to assume that everything
was settled. "I'll bring her back Monday morning,"

she said after Aunt Bea had given Julie a tour of the apartment, showing her the bed she'd share with Terry, the empty dresser drawers where her clothes would go, the chair that would be hers at the dining-room table. Julie exposed her belly and rolled her eyes.

At the front door the social worker handed over a file, saying, "You might as well keep this."

"Oh, good," Aunt Bea said, as if the contents were familiar but she'd better have them just in case. When she was alone, she sat on the couch with a cup of coffee and the rest of the cookies and opened the file. How she would end up explaining Julie to people (to her daughter) was that she was floored by the coincidences, especially the coincidence of Julie's last name—Norman. "That was the clincher," Aunt Bea would say.

To see or hear her husband's name still threw weight on Aunt Bea's heart, but to see his name written next to that poor, forsaken girl's fogged up Aunt Bea's glasses. She touched under one eye, and she was crying all right. Before Norman died she wouldn't have believed it was possible to cry unbeknownst to yourself. Before Norman died she wouldn't have said that her glasses fogged from crying, although she didn't doubt that they had and she just couldn't remember. The most startling and depressing news in her life these days was what she was capable of forgetting. Well, she wouldn't forget the girl's last name, she could guarantee that. She removed her glasses, wiped them on her blouse and lifted her feet onto the coffee table.

The report was handwritten, hard to read. Under "Mother" it said either "Sally" or "Sandy" and then "38."

Then there was a short, tragic biography. Sally or Sandy
had an honours BA in English Literature but she also
had a drug habit and a long history of arrests for possession and trafficking. She was currently serving a five-
or an eight-year jail sentence. Her only other child had
been born addicted to heroin and had lived just a day.

As she read, Aunt Bea shook her head in pity and
amazement. It so happened that she had a cousin named
Sally, who used to teach school but who lost her husband and her job due to addiction to alcohol. She died
at age forty, a broken old woman.

"Heaven help her," Aunt Bea prayed for Julie's
mother.

Under "Father," all it said was "Michael, ill."

"Good heavens!" Aunt Bea said. He must be a stepfa-
ther, she thought. Or maybe he was the mother's father.
But still . . . ill. And then she let out a whoop of laugh-
ter as she realized that what it actually said was "Ill." She
laughed and laughed and had to remove her glasses and
wipe them again. When she settled down she got a little
irritated. What did they mean by "Ill"? Crazy? Dying?
Dying from AIDS which they didn't want to say in case
people were afraid to take Julie? Aunt Bea clicked her
tongue to imagine so much ignorance.

She turned the page, and there was another coincidence—Julie suffered from epileptic fits. Aunt Bea's
younger sister, dead thirty-four years now, had suffered
from epileptic fits. Aunt Bea was handy, therefore, with
a pencil. Get the tongue out of the way first, tilt back
the head. Nothing to be alarmed about, so long as there
were unsharpened pencils all over the house.

"Prone to temper tantrums," Aunt Bea read. "Domineering." She thought of her daughter and felt herself well prepared. "Behavioural and intellectual age," she read, "five to six." "Well . . . ," she said dubiously. She had been very impressed by Julie's detection of Sweet'n Low.

She told Terry the news that afternoon, on their walk home from school. It wasn't until she was actually describing Julie that she recognized what a burden she was asking Terry to share. This wasn't how she had planned it at all. The brain-damaged girl she found herself bracing Terry for was a far cry from the helpful and spirited older sister she'd had in mind. She tried to brighten up the picture. "We'll have a whale of a time, though," she said, "the three of us."

"Doing what?" Terry asked.

"Oh, I don't know . . ." Aunt Bea thought back to when her daughter was small. "We'll take the ferry to the island," she said, although being on boats gave her heart palpitations.

Terry swept her white cane in scrupulous arcs.

"And we'll go to the zoo," Aunt Bea said, although the zoo was a good fifty miles away, and Aunt Bea no longer drove a car.

"Where will she sleep?" Terry asked.

"With you. If that's all right. It's a big enough bed."

"What if she wets her pants? A boy at school who is five, he wets his pants."

"In that department, I'm sure she's eleven," Aunt Bea said, although she thought, Good point, and wondered if she shouldn't lay some plastic garbage bags under the sheet.

"Will she go to school?"

"She already goes. That school on Bleeker. You know, where the sidewalk's all cracked?"

"Will she go by herself?"

"No, I don't think so. We'll both walk her there, and then I'll take you to school."

Terry came to a stop and lifted her thin face in Aunt Bea's direction. "Your feet will kill you!" she cried, as if delivering the punch line.

"Lord," Aunt Bea said. "Lord, you're right."

Julie is holding Aunt Bea's left hand. Terry is holding Aunt Bea's right hand. The three of them take up the whole sidewalk, and oncoming people have to step out onto the road. Julie is thrilled by this, believing, as she does, that it is happening because she does not smell afraid. "Bastards and dogs can smell it when you're afraid," her mother told her. So Julie is walking with her head lowered to butt. Whenever somebody veers off the sidewalk she murmurs, "Bastard."

Eventually Aunt Bea asks, "Where's the fire?" She thinks that Julie is saying, "Faster."

"Dog," Julie says quietly—this time it's a dog that has trotted onto the road. She laughs and pulls up her dress.

"No!" Aunt Bea says.

"No!" Terry echoes, recognizing the familiar sound of Aunt Bea slapping Julie's clothing down.

"Oh-kay, oh-kay," Julie says.

"Not now," Terry says. Sometimes Julie and Terry play a game that Julie made up, where Julie chants oh-kay, oh-kay while she and Terry hold hands and swing their arms back and forth, just a bit at first, and then higher and higher until they swing them right around over their heads. Terry isn't crazy about this game, but she plays it to calm Julie. She thinks that Julie is probably blue with lines. Aunt Bea is green. Blood is red.

Aunt Bea gives them each a Life Saver, then takes their hands. The sweeps of the white cane along the sidewalk strike Aunt Bea as a blessing, a continuous sanctification of their path. "I want you both to be angels in church," she says. "It's a special day."

"I know," Terry says importantly.

Julie sucks her Life Saver and rubs Aunt Bea's wrist against her cheek.

"Do you know what?" Terry says.

"What?" Aunt Bea says.

"Julie poked the eyes out of her doll." The hole in her Life Saver has reminded her.

"Yes, I saw that," Aunt Bea says.

Julie isn't paying attention. She is remembering her mother's phone call and is daydreaming about her mother singing "Six Little Ducklings." Julie smiles at her mother, which provokes Aunt Bea, who after a year still gets Julie's smiles and grimaces confused, to say, "Listen, *I* don't give a hoot. It's *your* doll. If you want to destroy it, that's up to you."

"Just don't expect a new one!" Terry cries.

"That's right," Aunt Bea says.

"My mother has left the jail," Julie says.

"What?" Aunt Bea comes to a stop.

"She phoned yesterday. She told Penny."

"No, she didn't!" Terry cries. Her shrill laugh shoots a pain through Aunt Bea's eyes.

"Yes, she did," Julie says slowly and murderously.

"It's so funny!" Terry cries. She yanks her hand from Aunt Bea's and pats the air in an excited manner. She is wearing white felt gloves. "You know how she always says it's her mother on the phone? Well, do you know what? Yesterday the phone rang when you were in the laundry room, and I answered it, and it was a woman, and she said, 'This is Sally, is Marge . . .' or somebody . . . yes, it was Marge. She said, 'This is Sally, is Marge there?' And I said she had the wrong number, and then I told Julie, and she said that her mother's name is Sally."

"That's right," Aunt Bea says. "It is."

"It is," Julie says, scowling at Terry.

"But it's so funny!" Terry cries. The strap of her white plastic purse falls down her shoulder. She reaches for it and drops her cane. "No!" she screams, imagining that the dog Julie mentioned a minute ago is racing to retrieve it.

Aunt Bea picks the cane up. "Honey, that was *another* woman named Sally," she says to Julie.

Julie bunches the skirt of her dress and rolls her eyes.

"I *told* her," Terry says.

"But your mother will be out of jail one day," Aunt Bea says, tugging down Julie's dress. "And until then

Penny and I want you to live with us."

Julie's face empties. She has been dazed, suddenly, by a recollection of the woman who knelt over the cat that fell from the balcony, by a recollection of the woman's black-and-white dress, exactly like her mother's. She reasons that the woman was in jail before and is now out.

"Okie dokie?" Aunt Bea says.

Julie covers her mouth with both hands, the way the woman did.

"Okie dokie," Aunt Bea answers for her.

In the middle of the sermon Aunt Bea is visited by the notion that the reason Julie calls Terry "Penny" might be that somebody, her educated mother for instance, told her about the pennies that used to be put on the eyes of the dead who, of course, can no longer see.

She gives Julie a ruminating look. Julie looks blankly back at her and begins to jerk. Before Aunt Bea understands what is happening, she kicks the pew. She swings her arm and knocks Aunt Bea's glasses off.

"Stop it!" Terry says to Julie. Aunt Bea's glasses have landed in her lap. She holds them over Julie, who has gone stiff and is slipping off the pew. Aunt Bea snatches her glasses back. "She pretending!" Terry says. "She's jealous."

"Shush!" Aunt Bea snaps. Julie begins jerking again. Aunt Bea pours out the contents of her purse but she can't find the pencil. Finally she shoves a hymnal into Julie's mouth, then throws her leg up and over Julie's to stop her kicking the pew, at which point she becomes aware that Hazel Gordimer is leading Terry into the aisle, and that Tom Alcorn, the minister, is asking if there's a doctor in the congregation. "It's all right," Aunt Bea calls out. "This happens all the time! It'll be over in a jiffy!" She smiles at the stricken faces turned toward her. She knows it looks worse than it is. Luckily, though, it's a short fit. With a mighty heave, Julie relaxes her body, and Aunt Bea calls out to Tom Alcorn, "All finished! You can carry on now!" She looks around for Terry, but she's not there—Hazel must have taken her outside. So she throws everything back in her purse, tugs the hymnal from Julie's mouth and coaxes her to her feet. "Sorry," she says to the people along the pew. "Thank you so much," she says, referring to their prayers for Terry.

The last man in the aisle, a big man about her age, takes her arm and walks her and Julie to the back of the church. In the silence can be heard, clear as a bell, the Sunday school children down in the basement singing "All Things Bright and Beautiful." Normally, Terry and Julie would be down there, but the topic of this Sunday's service, "Suffer Little Children," was dedicated to Terry, and Aunt Bea wanted her to hear it. Well, she heard most of it. She heard her name mentioned in two prayers. Aunt Bea runs a hand over her pounding forehead, and the man, whose name she wishes she could remember, gives her arm a squeeze. Oh, the consolation of big, church-going men! Aunt Bea allows herself to lean into him a little. Julie leans into her. Aunt Bea looks down at her and sees what she knows in her bones is a smile.

At the door the man draws his arm away, and the three of them go outside and descend the steps toward Hazel Gordimer and Terry. Terry's eyelids are pink from crying. Suddenly Aunt Bea can't bear it that those tender lids will feel the scalpel. Letting go of one child, she goes up to the other and hugs her.

"She didn't make the sink-draining noise," Terry says coldly. "She always makes it first."

Aunt Bea is unable to recall whether Julie made that noise or not. "It was bad timing, I'll grant you that," she says. Terry wrenches free and begins to sweep the sidewalk with her cane. "Where are you going?" Aunt Bea asks. Terry approaches the man, who makes way, and then Julie, who doesn't. Terry has anticipated this, however, and she steps onto the grass one sweep before her cane would have touched Julie's shoe.

"Bastard," Julie murmurs.

"I *heard* that!" Terry says. At the stairs to the church she stops, confused—she thought she was heading in the other direction.

"Are you going back in?" Aunt Bea asks.

Terry doesn't know. She starts crying again—high, puppy-like whimpers that plunge Julie into grief and start her crying, too.

"Here we go," Aunt Bea sighs, walking over to Terry.

"Julie is stupid," Terry says.

"Oh, now," Hazel Gordimer admonishes.

"Julie has rocks in her head," Terry says.

Two days later Terry goes into the hospital. She is supremely confident. At the admission desk she asks if anyone knows a blind girl who needs an almost brand-new cane.

Aunt Bea is confident, too. The same doctor has been monitoring Terry ever since she was born, and he says she is the optimum age for the operation. He calls it a delicate but routine procedure with an extremely high success rate. "The only real worry I have," he says, "is how Terry will react to suddenly being able to see. There are always adjustment problems."

"You mean the birthmark," Aunt Bea says, getting down to brass tacks. Even though the doctor has explained to Terry how next year a plastic surgeon is going to erase the birthmark with a laser beam ("erase"—that's the word he used, as if somebody had spilled purple ink on her cheek), Aunt Bea doesn't exactly expect Terry to jump for joy the first time she looks in a mirror.

But the doctor says, "Spacial problems. An inability, in the beginning anyway, to judge depth and distances."

"Oh, well," Aunt Bea says. She has spacial problems herself, if that's the case. When she used to drive she had an awful time pulling out into traffic.

The church has arranged for a private hospital room, and members of the congregation have already filled it with flowers. Terry is exhilarated, Aunt Bea is touched, but when Aunt Bea has to go home, and Terry is lying down waiting for her dinner tray, all those bouquets surrounding that little body on the bed make Aunt Bea uneasy. Right after supper, leaving the dirty dishes on the table, she rushes back. She brings Julie this time, plus a big bag of chocolate-chip cookies, which, despite the flowers, Terry immediately smells. "I can't eat those!" she cries.

"You can't?" Aunt Bea says.

Terry gives her head the single nod that, for her, means absolutely not. "I can't eat anything till the operation. I have to have an empty stomach."

"Oh, that's right," Aunt Bea says, annoyed with herself. You'd have thought that after all of Norman's operations she'd have remembered.

Julie is still in the doorway. Although she hasn't said anything yet, Terry is aware of her. "Why are you just standing there?" she asks.

"Come on, honey, come over here and help me wolf some of these down," Aunt Bea says, dropping onto the chair and digging into the bag of cookies.

"Can Penny see?" Julie asks in her loud voice.

"Of course not!" Terry cries. "I haven't even had the operation yet!"

"In a week, Penny will be able to see," Aunt Bea says. She hoists her sore feet onto the radiator.

Julie scowls and sticks a finger in her ear. She pushes so hard that she groans.

"What's the matter?" Aunt Bea says. "Come on over here."

Julie stays where she is. She is mentally scanning Aunt Bea's apartment. She sees the hammer and nails in an apple basket on the broom-closet floor. She sees the two screwdrivers in a juice can. She moves to the bedroom and sees the hangers in the bedroom closet, and she lingers there as she remembers her mother straightening out a hanger and poking it up a hash pipe once.

Despite her bandage, Terry is sure that she is already detecting the colour red. "It's very bright," she says. "It could hurt you, even."

Colours are all she talks about. For the first time in her life she wonders what colour writing is.

"Black," Aunt Bea says. "Nine times out of ten."

Terry can't understand how it is visible in that case— she can't grasp the idea of black against white, and Aunt Bea finally gives up trying to explain. "You'll see," she says.

"*I'll* see!" Terry loves saying this. She thinks it's the cleverest joke. *She'll* see—everything will become clear to her in a few days. She takes it for granted that she will know how to read as soon as she opens a book.

She also takes it for granted that people will want to adopt her, now that she's "normal." Aunt Bea is wounded by the eagerness in her voice. In a cautiously optimistic tone she says, "They probably will." Aunt Bea realizes, of course, that more couples will be interested, but there are still the adjustment problems that the doctor mentioned. And there's the birthmark, not just the first, startling sight of it, but having to deal with the laser-beam operation and its aftermath—expensive lotions or infections or whatever. In Aunt Bea's experience, there's always something. She can't help feeling the faintest breath of relief when she takes into account the birthmark. She hugs Julie and says, "Don't you worry. Penny will be back home before you know it."

Julie says, "Can Penny see yet?"

She asks every ten minutes. She is also suddenly obsessed by Terry's mother. Whenever they pass a woman in the hall of their apartment building—even a woman she knows—she asks, "Is that Penny's mother?"

"How many times have I told you?" Aunt Bea says, and this becomes another worry, not Julie's questions (who can hope to fathom what goes on in that child's damaged head?) but her own impatience with them. To strengthen herself she sings "Onward, Christian Soldiers." One night she falls into such a swamp of pity over Julie's childhood that she gets out of bed and sews her a dress out of the green velvet and white silk she'd intended to make Terry a dress out of. But when she presents the dress to Julie the next morning, Julie plants her fists on her hips and says, "Throw it in the garbage." So Aunt Bea cuts the threads and turns the dress into Terry's after all. She takes it to the hospital, her intention all along being that when the bandage is removed Terry should see the colour she has decided will be her favourite.

The doctor leads Terry to a chair and asks her to sit. Aunt Bea sits at the edge of the sofa.

"I just hope the blinds are closed," Terry says.

"They are." The doctor laughs.

"She doesn't miss a trick, that one," Aunt Bea says, leaning forward to smooth Terry's dress. She regrets the white sash and trim—she thinks they give the impression that she had bandages on the brain. She startles herself by letting out an explosive sob.

"It's so gloomy in here," the nurse says sympathetically.

"Are you crying?" Terry asks. "What are you crying for?"

Aunt Bea extracts a wad of kleenex from the sleeve of her sweater. "I always cry at miracles," she says. She squeezes Terry's bony knee. Terry is so keyed up that her legs are sticking straight out like a doll's. She tucks them in fast, however, when the doctor asks if she's all set. He moves a stool in front of her, sits, then signals to the nurse, who turns a dial on the wall.

The room darkens. Everything white seems to leap out—his gown, the silk, the bandage, the moons of his fingers touching the bandage. Aunt Bea looks at the moons in her own fingers, at the kleenex. She glances up at the light, wondering if it has a special bulb. On the far wall are staves of light from the gaps between the venetian blinds.

"Oh," Terry says.

The bandage is off.

The whites of her eyes are so white.

"Do your eyes hurt?" the doctor asks.

Terry blinks. "No," she whispers. The doctor waits a moment, then raises his hand a fraction and the nurse turns the dial.

"Angels," Terry says. All she can see are dazzling slashes and spots.

Aunt Bea is overcome. "Oh, dear Lord," she sobs.

"That is light," the doctor says.

"I know," Terry agrees. Now the slashes and spots

aren't so brilliant, and she is beginning to make out shapes filled in with what she realizes must be colour. Between the coloured shapes there is black.

"What else do you see?" the doctor asks.

"You," she whispers, but it is an assumption.

"What did she say?" Aunt Bea asks, wiping her fogged-up glasses.

"She sees me."

"I see you," Terry says, and now she does. That is his face. It grows, it comes closer. He is staring into one of her eyes and then the other. He is pulling down on her bottom lids. She stares back at his eyes. "An eye is greasy," she says.

When he moves his hand away, she looks down at her dress, then over at Aunt Bea, who isn't green. More startling than that, Aunt Bea's face is different from the doctor's. Men must have different faces from women, she thinks, but when she looks at the nurse, *her* face is different, too. The nurse is very tiny, only an inch high. Terry looks back at Aunt Bea and considers the gleaming lines between her eyes and her mouth. "I see your tears," she says.

"Oh, honey," Aunt Bea says.

Terry extends her hand, and though it seems to touch Aunt Bea, it doesn't. She waves it, and it brushes the doctor's face. "But—" she says, confused.

"That's what I was telling you about," the doctor says to Aunt Bea. "It's going to take her a while to judge distances." He turns to the nurse. "Let's open the blinds."

The nurse goes over to the window. Terry watches her. She expands as she approaches Terry, shrinks as she moves to the other side of the room. This is no surprise—Terry has always figured that certain people are big close up and little far away. But she had no idea that you could see behind you, that what was behind you remained visible. She twists back and forth to try to catch the space behind her in blackness.

"Stand up, why don't you," the doctor says.

Terry comes to her feet and faces the window.

"That's sky and clouds at the top part," the doctor says. "Blue sky, white clouds, and trees underneath, the green leaves of trees. These windows are tinted, so it's all a bit darker than it is really."

Terry takes a step. She stops, certain that she has reached the window. She holds out her hand, and Aunt Bea jumps up and grabs it. "Oh, honey," she says. It's all she can say.

"No." Terry says sharply, shaking Aunt Bea away. She feels better with her hand out in front of her. She takes two more steps, but she is still not at the window. Two more steps, two more. The nurse moves aside. Two more steps, and Terry's fingers hit the glass.

It is her hand that arrests her, pressed flat against the pane. "What are those cracks?" she says, referring to the wrinkles on her knuckles.

Aunt Bea is beside her. She scans the view outside. "On the building?" she asks, wondering if Terry means the lines between the bricks. "Over there?"

"No!" Terry slaps the window. She is suddenly panicky. "Where is Julie?" she says.

"At school," Aunt Bea says, putting an arm around her. "You know that, honey. You'll see her at home."

"Where's my face?" Terry says, and starts to cry.

"Okay," the doctor says. "It's a little overwhelming, isn't it, Terry?" He tells her to sit down and close her eyes. Whenever she is overwhelmed, he says, she should close her eyes for a few moments.

Terry targets the couch. She waves her hands to keep Aunt Bea from helping. She has the impression that she is walking into a picture of flat shapes and that the heat she senses radiating from Aunt Bea's body is what's causing the shapes to gradually melt from view.

Terry's hand is on her reflection in the bathroom mirror.

"That's coming off, remember," Aunt Bea says. "It'll be the same colour as the rest of your skin."

Terry's hand moves from the mirror to the fair side of her face. With the tips of her fingers she dabs herself, making what strike Aunt Bea as oddly haphazard leaps from cheekbone to jawbone to eyebrow, nose, mouth and then to the other side of her face—her cheek—where she halts for a moment.

She begins to smooth the skin there—she is testing if the birthmark wipes off. "You know what?" she says.

"What?"

"I love purple," she says wistfully.

"So do I!" Aunt Bea exclaims.

"But I thought purple would be green," Terry says. She turns her head as if her eyes were in danger of falling out. Her eyes look completely different since the operation. They seem smaller . . . and older—they have the vague intensity that reminds Aunt Bea of old people listening to something difficult and new.

"Would you like to see more purple?" Aunt Bea asks.

Terry's eyes fix on Aunt Bea's left hand. "Do you know what?" she says. "I thought veins would be red."

On the bus ride home, behind oversized sunglasses to eliminate glare, Terry had studied the veins in Aunt Bea's hands. Every few minutes she carefully lifted her head to look at the other passengers and at the ads above the windows, but she didn't look out the windows, although once or twice she caught sight of her dim reflection, she recognized the movement of her own head, and the first time this happened she said, alarmed, "That's a mirror!"

Between these investigations, she had returned to her real interest—examining the back of Aunt Bea's hand. As they were walking from the bus Aunt Bea showed her how when she held her hand up for a few moments all the veins disappeared, then when she brought it back down they re-emerged and made it seem as if she were ageing fifty years in five seconds. Terry loved that. "Again," she said. "Again."

As soon as they entered the apartment, however, she impatiently pushed away Aunt Bea's hand, looked down the hall and said, "The mirror over the sink, that's a real one, isn't it?"

"Yes," Aunt Bea said warily. In the hospital, despite asking where her face was, Terry had closed her eyes every time the doctor had tried to get her to look in a mirror. "Yes," Aunt Bea said. "That's a real mirror."

"Will you hold these?" Terry asked, taking off her

sunglasses. Then she made her way down to the bathroom.

Now she comes out into the hall, stops and shuts
her eyes. This is how she walks—stopping every five or
six steps to close her eyes and assume an expression of
beseeching concentration. Aunt Bea tries to get her to
put the sunglasses back on, but she says they turn off
the lights. Everywhere she sees lights. In the benjamina
plant, in Aunt Bea's hair, strips of light on a vase, squares
and spills of light that take Aunt Bea a moment and
some wilful hallucinating to discern.

Terry switches on the television. There is a face not
unlike the doctor's. It upsets her when Aunt Bea says
it's not him. Every time the picture changes she cries,
"What's that?" although she usually figures it out before
Aunt Bea answers. After about a quarter of an hour she
switches the TV off, saying, "It's too crowded." She wants
to see Julie, who is being walked home from school by a
neighbour.

"She'll be home at four o'clock," Aunt Bea says.

So she wants to see the kitchen clock. Aunt Bea re-
moves it from the wall and lets her hold it. "But where's
the time?" she cries, distressed.

It's the same with the Bible. "But I can't see what it
says," she cries. They are sitting on Aunt Bea's bed, the
Bible opened on Terry's lap to a page of all-red words,
which is Jesus speaking.

Aunt Bea says, "Of course you can't, honey."

Terry closes the Bible. With an air of respectful but
absolute dismissal she sets it on the bedside table. She
looks down at Aunt Bea's hands. "Show me your veins,"
she says.

They are still in the bedroom when the apartment door opens. "In here!" Aunt Bea calls, and suddenly Julie is standing in the doorway, with Anne Forbes, from down the hall, behind her.

"Hi!" Terry says in a dreamlike voice. She knows which one is Julie, and Julie so rivets her that Anne Forbes, a tall, horse-faced woman wearing gold hoop earrings and two green combs in her red hair, is nothing but an unfocused mass of colours.

"Can Penny see yet?" Julie asks.

"I see you," Terry says. "You have blue on."

"Well," Julie sighs. She glances back at Anne Forbes. "Your mother is here."

"Oh, my goodness!" Anne Forbes trills.

"That's Mrs. Forbes," Terry says. She recognizes the voice.

"Oh-kay, oh-kay," Julie says loudly.

"For heaven's sakes, Julie, you know that's Mrs. Forbes." Clutching the edge of the dresser, Aunt Bea pulls herself to her feet.

Julie throws her head back so that she is gaping into Anne Forbes's face. "Oh-kay, oh-kay," she shouts and rolls her eyes.

"Is it a fit?" Anne Forbes asks with a jittery laugh, stepping back.

"No, no," Aunt Bea says, "she's just a bit upset." She starts to go over to Julie, but Terry stands up and begins making her way there, so Aunt Bea stays where she is.

Terry crosses to the door without a halt. Her fingers

hit Julie's shoulder, and Julie, who seemed to be ignoring her, now looks at her and says, softly for Julie, "Oh-kay, oh-kay." She and Terry appear very engrossed, very dutiful as they clutch each other's hands and proceed to swing them back and forth.

There is no convincing Julie that the specialist who visits twice a week to help Terry adjust—a black woman no less—is not Terry's mother. She also can't seem to get it through her head that Terry no longer needs her to relate what's going on in the parking lot and playground next door.

"Red car," she says, and Terry glances out and says, "I know, I see it." In fact, Terry, who is making what the specialist calls astounding progress, adds, "It's a hatch-back."

"Hatch-back! Hatch-back!" Julie shouts, and continues shouting it and exposing her stomach and breasts until Terry bursts into tears.

"Julie feels abandoned," Aunt Bea explains to the woman from the newspaper, who happens to witness one of Julie's tantrums. "Of course," she adds, "Terry is high-strung."

"I can see that," the woman says. But in her "Everyone's Children" column, which advertises a different foster child each day, she decides that all she saw in terms of Terry's character was a "quick-witted, independent charmer . . . a friendly and cheerful chatterbox." After a morning of arguing with herself, Aunt Bea phones the columnist up and gives her a piece of her mind. "It's only fair to paint the whole picture," she says. "I mean, it's not like there's a money-back guarantee."

"At this early stage," the columnist says, "the strategy is to stir up interest."

The interest of three couples is stirred up. For one reason or another, though, they all change their mind before even paying Terry a visit. Aunt Bea's heart breaks over these near misses, and yet she also feels as if she's been granted an eleventh-hour reprieve, and consequently she experiences attacks of guilt, such bitter attacks that she writes Ann Landers a letter signed "Possessive in Port Credit." Since she asks for a confidential response she doesn't really expect an answer—it was just a case of getting a load off of her chest. Just the same, she checks the newspaper every day, and a month later, lo and behold, there's a two-sentence response for "Possessive in P.C.," which Aunt Bea assumes must be her despite the fact that the message doesn't really add up. "Get the egg off your face, yokel," it says. "Do yourself a favour and seek counselling pronto."

What Aunt Bea does instead—what she's been doing all along —is get down on her knees and pray, three and four times a day, dimpling her forearms on the chenille coverlet she hasn't washed since Norman died because she believes she can still detect his body odour in it. Also she gives herself a penance—grateful dedication to Julie. When Terry is glued to the television or leafing through the piles of magazines the specialist brings over, Aunt Bea and Julie go down to the swings. Aunt Bea has to laugh at the two of them flailing their legs like beetles on their backs, a pair of fatsos in danger of bringing the whole set crashing down onto their heads. After a few minutes, though, Julie squirms off her swing to give Aunt Bea a push. She'd rather push than be pushed, and Lord knows she's as strong as an ox, and as dogged. If she could, she'd stand there pushing Aunt Bea all day. She pushes her so high that the chains buckle and Aunt Bea cries out.

It is always a surprise to Julie every time the specialist leaves without taking Terry with her. Then she remembers that there is a bad man over at Terry's mother's house, that's why. He's the same man who punched Julie's mother and drowned the cat in the toilet.

"When the man goes to jail," she assures Terry, "your mother will take you home."

"I don't have a mother!" Terry cries.

"When the man goes . . . ," Julie says, nodding. Her faith in this is invincible.

She waits for her own mother to show up. She rushes to answer the phone and the buzzer, often persuading herself that it *is* her mother in the lobby, so that when it's only Anne Forbes, or the specialist, or somebody else, she is incredulous. She hurries over to the window, hoping to catch sight of her mother walking away. She thinks that what happened was, her mother changed her mind. She throws herself into a fit. She swats at Aunt Bea. One day, while Aunt Bea is talking to someone out in the hall, she snatches Aunt Bea's blue sweater from the back of her chair and drops it out the window. A minute later Terry emerges from the bathroom, leans out the window and cries, "There's a little lake down there!"

"Lake! Lake!" Julie mocks her. It enrages her when Terry makes these errors. A sweater is not a lake! Terry's mother will get mad! With her shirt up around her neck, Julie struts around the living room, enraged and growing brave. Before Aunt Bea manages to get away from her visitor, Julie has gone into the kitchen, taken a chopstick out of the cutlery drawer and stabbed it through a plastic placemat.

"No!" Terry screeches.

Julie holds the placemat up. "Oh-kay, oh-kay," she says, disappointed. The hole is so small she can't even poke her finger through.

Terry sees things that Aunt Bea has never seen before or has forgotten having seen. When the subway is leaving the station, Terry thinks it's the platform not the subway that is moving. She sees the spokes of bicycle wheels rotating in the opposite direction than they actually are. She sees faces in the trunks of a tree. The bark of a tree she compares to the back of Aunt Bea's hand. She says, "The sky comes right down to the ground"—they are standing on the shore of the lake at the time—and Aunt Bea thinks, It's true, the sky isn't up there at all. It is all around us. We are *in* the sky.

"You are the Lord's little visionary," she tells Terry.

Sometimes she is happy just to be alive and a witness. Sometimes she wants to run off with both girls to a desert island. "Why aren't I adopted yet?" Terry occasionally asks, not so much wounded as puzzled. "It takes time" is Aunt Bea's lame answer, but as the weeks pass and no more couples make inquiries, she begins to suppose that it really does take time. She begins to lose some of her awful anxiety and guilt.

The days settle around her, each blessed, hard-won day. She believes she is reaping the reward of prayer—she can sense the Lord in the apartment, keeping tabs on her blood pressure. She tugs down Julie's shirt and slaps down Julie's slapping hands and is no more upset than if she was hanging laundry on a windy day and the sheets were pelting her head. She remembers her own daughter's tantrums at this age, her cruel tongue, and she tells Terry, "This is nothing. This won't hurt you."

One day, though, when Julie is stomping around the living room, the picture over the couch—an oil painting of two Scotty dogs exactly like Angus and Haggis, the litter-mates she and Norman used to have—comes crashing down, ripping away a chunk of plaster and missing Terry, who is looking at a magazine on the floor, by a fraction of an inch.

After the first seconds of silence following Terry's scream, Aunt Bea turns to Julie and says, "Bad girl." She is so angry that her jaw trembles.

Julie throws herself on the floor and begins to punch herself in the head.

"Bad," Aunt Bea says. A sob leaps to her throat.

Terry is kneeling over the painting. It has landed face down and she seems to be trying to dig her fingers under the frame.

"Don't do that!" Aunt Bea snaps.

"But where's their backs!" Terry cries. "Where's the back of them?"

Aunt Bea has no choice except to call Fred, the superintendent, to fix the plaster. She hates doing this because Fred always acts rudely interrupted and because the first time Terry saw him after the operation, she said, "I thought you would have hair." But Fred says, "Christ, I guess I better take a look at it," and arrives with powdered plaster, which he mixes in Aunt Bea's cut-glass salad bowl. When he's done he makes Aunt Bea come out of the bathroom so that he can hold the nail up before her eyes. "You mean to tell me you were using this?" he says.

Aunt Bea fails to understand.

"You can't hang a picture that size with a half-inch nail. You got to use a screw. Drill a hole, stick in a wall plug."

"Oh, I see." Aunt Bea pats her heart. "Could you do that for me, Fred?" She doesn't own a drill. She has palpitations and gas. She has just remembered that it's her wedding anniversary. She can't get Julie, who is still lying on the floor, grimacing wildly, to so much as glance at her.

"The plaster's wet," Fred says, as if she's an idiot.

"When it's dry then," Aunt Bea says.

"I haven't got all day," he says. "I'll do it now, a couple of inches over from where you had it. Doesn't look like it was centred on the wall anyway."

He comes back with a drill. Terry covers her ears when he turns it on, but Julie scrambles to her feet and stands right next to him, so close that he lifts his elbow and orders her to back up. A few seconds later he says, "Christ, now look what you made me do." He's drilled a hole too big for the plugs he has in his pocket.

He goes back down to the basement. Terry accompanies him to the elevator so that she can press the button. Aunt Bea goes into the bathroom to take more antacid.

Julie picks up the drill.

She doesn't scream, she doesn't make a peep. When Aunt Bea hears the whirring, all she thinks is, That was fast. She comes out of the bathroom just as Terry disappears into the living room.

Terry's scream is as high and clean as a needle.

"Oh, dear," Aunt Bea says, because she doesn't know yet what she is seeing. Julie's head jerks, as if she is sneezing. Red paint drips from her forehead. She holds the drill in both hands. Fred's drill—that's what's upsetting to Aunt Bea. Fred's paint.

Terry screams again. Right into Julie's head the scream goes, right into the hole where Julie's finger is going. Aunt Bea brings down the knick-knack holder on her way to the floor.

Everybody reassures Aunt Bea. The doctor pokes rods into a rubberized brain to demonstrate the harmless route the drill bit took and the dozen other harmless routes it might have taken. The child psychologist says that nothing short of boring the hole and sticking her finger in it was probably going to convince Julie there weren't rocks in her head. The social worker says that Julie's mother has been stunned into realizing that her parental responsibilities don't end at a cell door. Another social worker, the one who takes Julie to the group home, says that Julie should have been living with mentally disabled children all along.

But Aunt Bea doesn't let herself off the hook. When Terry leaves for school she starts remembering things that Julie said and did. Every gesture, every word seems to be a clue. Aunt Bea is appalled by the multitude of clues.

She is resigned to having Terry taken away from her as well. She is almost glad. Her daughter is right—she is too old for this, and it could have been a lot worse. When a social worker she doesn't know phones to ask if she is interested in another girl, she suspects it's a mixup and starts explaining who she is and what happened. But the social worker has heard all about it and blames Children's Aid.

"This new girl is bright," the social worker says. "The only thing is, she's missing both arms just above the elbow. She's in the process of being fitted with new artificial arms, though, and very sophisticated mechanical hands."

At supper that night, Aunt Bea tells Terry. "We don't have to have her," she says. "I'm happy enough just with you."

"I'd love to see a girl without arms!" Terry cries.

"If she lived here," Aunt Bea says, "it would involve more than just seeing her arms."

"Would her artificial arms come off?"

"I imagine so." Aunt Bea strokes the purple side

of Terry's face. The birthmark is being "erased" in a month.

Terry takes Aunt Bea's hand and lifts it up. "Show me your veins," she says.

Aunt Bea holds her hand over her head for a minute, then puts it on the table. The blue rivulets emerge as if the hand is under an evil maiden-to-crone spell.

"Too bad I can't go around with my hands up in the air all the time," Aunt Bea says.

"You know what?" Terry cries. Her feverish, old-woman gaze still startles Aunt Bea a bit when it fixes on her.

"What?"

"Too bad you can't go around with your whole body up in the air!"

The girl's name is Angela; she is twelve years old. She is perky, pretty (long black hair, flirtatious brown eyes), and she performs a tap-dance routine to "Singing in the Rain," which she has on a cassette tape.

Terry is enraptured. Aunt Bea is too, but not so much because of the dance—her daughter took tap-dancing lessons. What wins Aunt Bea's heart is the sight of those two little wing-like arms flapping at one of her artificial arms (she insists on putting them on her herself), flapping and failing to grasp it, flapping and failing, and at last lining it up, slipping the stump into the socket, and clicking it in.

SYLVIE

ALTHOUGH Sylvie draws a blank about what happened to her before her first day of school, her absolute recollection of certain moments *after* that day is a documented medical marvel. She doesn't just remember verbatim conversations, she remembers how the air smelled and if there was a breeze. She remembers that while her mother waited for her father to answer, a train whistled far off and there were mice scratching in the walls. If there were three dead flies on the windowsill and she noticed them ten years ago, she notices them again in her memory. "It's like dreaming when you know it's a dream," she tells the fat lady, Merry Mary. "You've got two lives going on at once."

"As if," Merry Mary points out, "*you* don't anyways."

Merry Mary is referring to the fact that Sylvie's Siamese twin sister, Sue, is attached to her. Sue is nothing but a pair of legs, though. Perfect little legs with feet, knees, thighs, hips and a belly, the belly growing out of Sylvie's own belly, just under her navel, and the feet hanging to a few inches below her own knees and facing away from her body, that is to say, facing in the same direction as her own feet. She has no more will over these little legs than she does over her ears, but she feels them, the cramps they occasionally get, the twitches, anything touching them. Off and on during the day she holds them by the feet and bends and stretches them, a habit drilled into her by her mother, who said that otherwise they would rot and fall off.

The school nurse eventually told Sylvie that this wasn't true. "No such luck," was how the nurse put it, in spite of which she encouraged exercises to control the cramps. She also set Sylvie straight regarding her mother's conviction that if she hadn't been constipated throughout the pregnancy, there would have been enough room inside her for two babies to grow.

"Malarkey," the nurse said.

"I thought so," Sylvie murmured. But she went right on suffering survivor guilt.

Sylvie never had reason to believe that her mother was upset about having a daughter with an extra pair of legs. The reason her mother sighed over everyone else's good luck and made sarcastic remarks about their supposed problems was that she had a daughter who was nothing but legs. She knit blue-and-white or red-and-white striped stockings for Sue (Sylvie had to wear plain white) and bought her new shoes (Sylvie's were second-hand, from the church bazaar). As if Sylvie weren't there, as if she weren't the one who felt what Sue felt, her mother squeezed Sue by her feet and massaged her calves and said, "How's my baby? What kind of day did my sweet baby have?" By Sue's round knees her mother said you could tell that she would have taken after her side of the family, the Scottish, blonde, plump side.

"These," her mother said, knocking on Sylvie's own bony knees, "are Portuguese."

Her mother's obvious favouritism hurt Sylvie, but at the same time she felt sorry for her sister, and she appreciated her own good fortune in having an entire body, plus, at her sister's expense, a second pair of legs, which, even if they didn't work, no one else had. Given her mother's behaviour, the last thing Sylvie suspected was that the legs were alarming. There was nobody to tell her. She was an only child, and her father, who worked long shifts in a light-bulb factory and was hardly ever at home, didn't speak fluent enough English to say much. They lived at the end of a deeply rutted dirt road on a piece of poor land where German shepherds ran loose. Maybe Sylvie went to town a few times before starting school, she doesn't remember. A year could go by without a visitor.

The school inspector must have visited. They had no phone, so people had to come by in person to tell them anything. Her mother subsequently referred to the inspector as That Man, and when he died, a year later, she said that if they thought she was going to wax That Man's coffin they had another think coming.

Two days a week her mother cleaned at the funeral parlour for twenty dollars a month plus the wilted flower arrangements. On Sylvie's first day of school the red ribbons holding her pigtails were cut from a Rest-in-Peace sash, as was the white trim that at the last moment her mother sewed along the hem of her skirt to make sure her little legs didn't show.

Her mother took her to school the first day, in the

horse cart. Sometimes they owned a truck, but not that year. When the schoolhouse came into sight down the road, her mother said, "You keep Sue under your skirt. Don't show her to anybody. Don't exercise her until you're back home."

Sylvie was standing in the cart to see over her mother's shoulder. "Are they playing tag?" she asked rapturously as the children stopped playing and cried "Here she is!" and "It's her!" and ran out onto the road.

"Sit down," her mother said.

The cart creaked and clacked up to the school. With a pang Sylvie noticed that all of the girls' skirts were shorter than hers and that none of the girls had pigtails. Her mother drove about twenty yards past the children before stopping. "Go right inside," she said. Her eyes were on a boy who was off by himself, smoking a cigarette.

Sylvie picked up her lunch pail and climbed out. When she reached the children they parted to make a path. The look on some of the children's faces made her instinctively shield the front of herself with her lunch pail, and yet she wasn't connecting her little legs to those looks. Her mother's warning to keep Sue under her skirt, she had taken to mean: don't be immodest, don't show off.

She was now at the schoolhouse steps. Holding the lunch pail pressed against her little legs, she turned and waved to her mother. Her mother snapped the reins, a sound Sylvie heard in her left ear, while in her right ear she heard a voice pitched like her own—her first experience of another little girl speaking to her.

"Can we see them?" the girl asked.

"See what?" Sylvie said.

"Your legs."

"My mother said I'm not allowed to."

"Is that where they are?" a second girl asked, pointing at where Sylvie held the lunch pail. This girl had mean eyes and long teeth.

"I'm supposed to go right inside," Sylvie murmured, and she started to walk around the children.

Somebody tried to lift her skirt. When she swung around to see who, a hand darted in front of her, under her lunch pail, and smacked one of her little legs on the knee. "I felt them!" the mean-eyed girl screamed. A boy yanked Sylvie's hair. She let go of her lunch pail, and immediately the front of her skirt was under attack. "Don't!" she cried. Somebody pushed her, and she fell to the ground. Her skirt was pulled above her knees. Her arms were pinned, a hand clamped over her mouth. The hand smelled like tobacco. The children who could see gasped and fell silent. "I'm going to bring up," a girl whispered, and Sylvie thought that it was because of her underpants showing, hers and Sue's, but then a boy touched her little leg on the shin, a quick testing pressure with the ends of his fingers, and Sylvie got the picture—her little legs were white slugs when you turn over a rock.

When everyone had taken a look, some of the older girls helped her up. They swiped dirt from her skirt, careful to avoid the front of her. They examined the cut on her arm. It didn't need a bandage, they agreed. A girl who wore glasses picked up Sylvie's lunch pail and praised the strawberries painted on it. "Don't cry," she said. "They just looked like normal legs to me."

"It's your own fault," the mean-eyed girl rasped in her ear. "You should have showed us when we asked nicely."

That was the best advice Sylvie ever got. From then on, if anyone asked to see her legs, nicely or not, she hiked up her skirt. Kids brought their older brothers and sisters and their parents to the school yard to see her. One boy brought a blind aunt who, after gripping each of Sue's thighs, said, "Just as I thought. Fake. Plantation rubber."

It didn't take long for Sylvie's parents to find out what was going on. Sylvie's compliance was the thing that her mother couldn't get over. She called Sylvie a dirty dish rag. She said that a steady diet of scratches and pokes in the eye would have soon taught the children a lesson.

"But if I don't show them, they'll scratch and poke me," Sylvie said.

"Then that is your lot!" her mother shouted. "That is your cross to bear! Think of what Sue has borne! Think of what *I* have borne!"

At this point her father appeared from another room. "Why not she stay here?" he said.

"What?" Her mother looked startled by this rare intervention.

"You give her the lessons," he said.

"What?" her mother said louder.

"Like before." He shrugged.

"What did I tell you?" her mother shouted at him.
"What did That Man say? Truancy is against the law!
Against the law! Do you want us all hauled off to the
slammer?"

At dismissal the next afternoon her mother showed
up and laid into Sylvie's teacher, Miss Moote, for not
being on the ball. From then on, Miss Moote kept Sylvie inside at recess and waited with her outside the front
doors until her mother arrived in the cart. Tuesdays and
Fridays, the days her mother cleaned the funeral parlour,
her father was supposed to come for her, but more often
than not he got tied up at the factory, and finally Miss
Moote would walk around the school and say timidly
that all the children were long gone, she was sure it was
all right for Sylvie to walk home.

It was never all right. Boys ambushed her and poked
and tickled her little legs to see them kick. One day the
boy who chain-smoked stuck his finger up between both
pairs of her legs, her little ones and then her own, and
she had to race home to wash out the blood that dripped
onto her underpants.

She lay them in the warming oven to dry, but Sue's
pair, a higher-quality cotton than her own, were still
damp when she heard her mother opening the front
door. She had to put them on anyway (she and Sue
owned only one pair each) and just hope that her mother
wouldn't notice.

Not only did her mother not notice, she had a gift
from the funeral parlour. After stroking and massaging
Sue and asking about her day, she stood up, reached in
her coat pocket and withdrew a folded piece of paper.

"Found it beside Mr. Arnett on the slab," she said, un-wrapping the napkin to reveal a dead praying mantis. "Right beside his ear, like it was praying for his old skin-flint soul and then keeled over from the formaldehyde. Don't ask me how it got in there, though."

As Sylvie carefully picked the insect up, the boy's finger stabbing her and Sue became the darkness before the dawn, the terrible trial that had earned her this oth-erwise unaccountable blessing. The blessing wasn't just that Sylvie had never seen a real praying mantis, it was that her mother had been trying for months to find a buyer for the microscope. Her father, claiming to have got the microscope cheap at a fire sale, gave it to Syl-vie on her birthday. Ten dollars, her father finally con-fessed, and for a day Sylvie's mother muttered and raged that amount, and then she posted For Sale notices on telephone poles in town. But there were no takers, and meanwhile Sylvie used the microscope to study insects.

With the praying mantis, she began a collection. First she studied the insect from every possible angle, then, after flattening it with a rock or by rolling a pencil over it, she cleaned it off with vinegar and water. When it was dry she ironed it between pieces of wax paper and glued it into a scrapbook.

She filled three scrapbooks in three years. In her fourth scrapbook she branched out to include larvae and worms. By then she was identifying her catches with the help of a library book, and making labels from letters cut out of the Montgomery Ward catalogue. On the fac-ing page she would write down some aspect of what she had read or observed. "To defend itself the *catocala* hides its colourful wings with dull wings that blend in with the surroundings." "A black line under its back wings is the only difference between the Basilarchia butterfly and the monarch butterfly."

A few weeks after her fourteenth birthday she gave this activity up. One day she didn't have the heart to flatten another insect. Also she hardly ever discovered anything she didn't already have, and this frustrated her, especially as she knew that there were hundreds, maybe thousands, of different insect species right on her land alone.

The exciting feeling of the hunt didn't end, though. In fact, because of her memory spells, it came back to her at least once a week, as vividly as the real thing. Other moments came back as well (she had no control over what entered her mind at these times) but usually in her memory she was stalking or preserving one of her insects.

The spells had started a year before, and always when she was nervous or upset. Her mother would be yelling at her, and Sylvie would hear every word her mother said, and she'd see her mother there, banging a pot down, but why she squinted was from late-afternoon sun glancing off the barn roof, and why she felt an urge to lift her hand was that her hand *was* lifting, to pluck an aphid from the rose trellis. She heard her mother in the kitchen and heard her mother two years ago, calling from the barn door.

Even without her spells Sylvie had an excellent memory. She memorized her textbooks and got perfect grades and achievement pins. During spare periods and physical education classes (from which she was excused) she studied in the library or in an empty classroom. Since everyone who wanted to had seen her legs at least once, she was left alone.

In her junior year, however, an army base was set up down the road from the school, and cadets began to wait for her, two or three of them a day, outside the school gates. They took pictures of her to send to their families and to carry in their pockets—for good luck, they said, when they were shipped off to fight the war in Europe.

Sylvie didn't mind. The truth was, she had a soft spot for the cadets, who brought her chocolates and told her she looked like the movie star Vivien Leigh. They made jokes and teased her, but they did it to her face, there was no hypocritical pretense of sparing her feelings.

One day a carnival came to town, and not a single person from school had the nerve to tell her about the freak show, but the cadets did, no beating around the bush, straight to the Siamese-twin foetuses in a jar.

"Like you, except with four arms and another head," one of the cadets reported. "And dead, naturally. Can't hold a candle to you, though."

Sylvie turned on her heel and made for the Brown farm, where the carnival was set up. She found the sideshow tent by following red arrows that said "This Way For The Thrill of Your Life!" and "Keep Going Thrill Seekers!" Next to the tent was a big sign that said:

M. T. BEAN OF NEW YORK CITY PRESENTS
THE SIDE SHOW OF THE DECADE.

TALLEST, SMALLEST, THINNEST, FATTEST,
STRANGEST, RAREST EVER TO WALK
THE FACE OF THE EARTH!

Underneath was a painting of a thin man in a tuxedo,
a fat lady wearing a crown and sitting on a throne, and
a tall lady with huge hands holding out a plate that
had a midget standing on it. The foetuses weren't in the
painting.

"Next show in half an hour," a boy said. "You can
buy your ticket now. Fifty cents."

Sylvie didn't have any money, she hadn't thought
about having to pay admission. "I'll come back," she
said.

She was sure that her parents would want to see the
foetuses as badly as she did. She was wrong. An odd,
dark look came over her father's face. Her mother called.
M.T. Bean a vulture.

"But, Mother," Sylvie protested. "Siamese twins.
Like me and Sue."

"*Not* like you and Sue!" her mother cried, shaking
a ladle at her. "Naked! Meat on display! That's what I
saved you from!"

The next day Sylvie left home. She hadn't planned
to, but when she got to the fairgrounds and found the
tents gone, she started walking to New York City. She
remembered that Mr. Bean was from New York City.
She figured that by heading east and following road
signs, she'd eventually get there. In the back of her mind
she had a plan to exhibit herself at diners in exchange for
free meals and a place to sleep.

Three hours later she came upon the carnival in a meadow, not set up but with the trailers spread out and people lounging around drinking beer. A piebald Negro wolf-whistled at her.

"Is Mr. Bean here?" she asked him.

"Honey, you don't want to see the Bean man," he said. "We got two trailers broke down, and the Bean man be a mean man today."

"He'll want to see me," Sylvie said.

He sure did. He offered her his chair and a bottle of Coke. He said he knew her mother.

"My mother's dead," Sylvie told him. "So is my father."

Mr. Bean narrowed his eyes. "How old are you?"

"Almost eighteen."

"Can you prove it?"

"When I was born, it was in the papers."

He smiled. "Right," he said. "Let's have a look."

He was a fat bald man in an undershirt and suspenders and with an English accent. He had her take off Sue's shoes and stockings, and then he squeezed each bare leg along its length. "Can you move 'em?" he asked. "Bowels function?"

She signed a contract that afternoon. Five years, forty dollars a week, free room and board, a fifty-fifty split on wardrobe and prop expenses. A second big sign would be painted, featuring her alone and calling her The Incredible Girl-Boy. Sue would become Bill, and Sylvie would tell funny stories about the trials and tribulations of being attached to a boy.

Sylvie and Merry Mary share a trailer. They've been sharing one for six years, from Sylvie's first day, their only stretch apart being when Mary had a fling with Leopard Man, and Sylvie moved in with one of the barker women.

A baby came of Mary's affair, a surprise baby, since Mary had no idea she was pregnant until she started giving birth on her specially made toilet. Sylvie was in the trailer at the time, and she pulled the baby out while Mary grunted in mild discomfort and gripped the toilet's support bars. It was a girl. Tiny, normal. Perfect.

"Well, whaddaya know?" Mary laughed, and on the spot she named her Sue, after Sylvie's legs. Mr. Bean went into high gear, planning a wedding, printing flyers. But before the flyers were sent out, Sue turned blue and died.

"The fat lady don't cry," Mary said when Mr. Bean advised her to let it all out a couple of hours after Sue stopped breathing and Mary was still holding her. She gave her up only when supper arrived. After eating, she put on her crown for her act and said, "Easy come, easy go," to comfort Sylvie, who was crying into a pile of laundered diapers and having a memory spell about gluing down a gypsy moth.

It took weeks for Sylvie to stop crying. She couldn't understand why she and Mary and the other freaks were alive, and a perfectly formed baby was dead. The minute she'd laid eyes on Sue it had struck her that it was all right being deformed if deformity had to exist for there to be such perfection. Sue's death left her out of kilter. "It doesn't make sense," she kept saying. And Mary said, "It sure don't," and "That's life," and then she said, "Who said it's supposed to make sense?" and finally she told Sylvie to snap out of it.

Mary never shed a tear. She said she wouldn't, and she never did. Instead she gained another eighty pounds, mainly in her lower half.

Now, Mary can hardly walk twenty feet, and more than ever she badgers Sylvie to visit whatever town they happen to be in, to see what's going on and to tell her all about it. "Take a break," she says, referring to Sylvie's ability to pass for a normal. It gives Mary a charge that the freak everyone comes to see is the only freak who can go around without being seen.

At one time or another all of the freaks have asked Sylvie what it's like to pass. What it's *really* like. She knows that they want to hear how wonderful it is, because passing is their dream, but they also want to hear how strange, even unpleasant, it is, because passing is a dream that won't come true for them. The truth is, it's both things. On the one hand Sylvie loves the feeling of being like everybody else, which is to say like nobody in particular. On the other hand when she feels most like a freak is when she's getting away with not being one.

For one thing she isn't as inconspicuous as the other freaks like to think. Aside from the spectacle of the unfashionably long full skirt she wears to cover her legs, there's her resemblance to Vivien Leigh. Wherever she goes, men look at her. Of course, she discourages the advances of strange men, but one day, when she is hav-

ing lunch in a restaurant, a man at the next table isn't
the least bit put off by her fake wedding ring or by the
annoyed looks she gives him. He keeps smiling at her,
an oddly conspiratorial smile, and in her agitation Sylvie is pouring a mixture of hot mustard and water down
worm holes fourteen years ago while knocking over her
Coke right now.

The man is there in a second, offering his napkin and
introducing himself. Dr. John Wilcox.

Sylvie is trapped by him blocking her way. Trapped
by his man's body, his adoring eyes and all his questions.
She gives her name and is surprised to find herself admitting that the ring isn't really a wedding band. One
part of her mind is rinsing the burning worms in a jar of
water, and the other part is telling Dr. John Wilcox that
she works in the travel business. Considering the miles
under her belt, this isn't entirely a lie.

"I've got to leave," she keeps saying, but weakly. She
feels melted to her chair. Between her little legs there's a
soft ache, and she can't tear her eyes from his mouth. He
has a beautiful mouth, a rosebud, a cherub's mouth. He
has blond, curly hair. Seven years in show business and
how many men has she watched watching her? Enough
to know that ones like him aren't a dime a dozen.

Suddenly he is quiet. He lifts her hand from the table
and holds it for a few minutes, turning it around, studying it. When can he see her again? He can't, she answers,
she isn't what he thinks she is. No, not in love with anyone else, but not free . . . not what he thinks. Pressing
her purse against her little legs to keep them still, she
stands up and walks away.

A few hours later she is on stage. As usual she's deep into a memory spell while still managing to deliver her lines and to glance around at the audience and to see and register everything and take it into herself as if through lead-lined holes that circumvent veins, arteries and organs.

"When Bill feels the call of nature, what do I do? Step into the ladies' or the men's?" She waits for the laugh, gets it, waits for the laugh to die, goes on. Fifteen years ago her mother is vilifying a woman named Velma Hodge. "Fat, wall-eyed sow," her mother says. Coincidentally there's a woman in the audience who could be Velma's twin. In this woman's face is the blend of repulsion and attraction that is in every face, and in the smoky air between Sylvie and the faces is the exchange of her watching them watching her.

Everything is going back and forth, in and out like breath.

And then she spots blond, curly hair, and it's as if a hypnotist snapped his fingers. Her mother's voice clears out of her head. All Sylvie hears is her own voice giving its spiel. "I tried to put a girl's pair of stockings on Bill, but he started kicking up such a fuss that I couldn't pull them up." She feels a mystifying desertion, a snapping of links.

Backstage she sits on a crate as the shock lifts and an old agony presses down. "I can help you," says a voice. It's him. Dr. John Wilcox. The worm memory resumes. She is squashing the life out of the worms, using the cut-off end of an old broomstick.

Dr. John Wilcox kneels and takes her right hand in his. He says she will leave this place tonight. She will stay

in his house. She never has to work in a side show again.
He will consult with surgeons about an operation, he
will take her anywhere in the world for an operation. He
loves her. The minute he saw her he knew, and he only
loves her more now. He wants to marry her.

It is a miracle too big to question. What Sylvie questions are the particulars. Don't worry, he says. Never
worry again. Her contract he will buy out. Her friends
she can visit. So while he goes to talk to Mr. Bean, she
goes to tell Merry Mary the news. "Holy moly," is all
Mary can say. "Holy moly."

John has a housekeeper and a cook, both late-mid-
dle-aged women, polite and unruffled by Sylvie showing up. Her bedroom is next to his, and that night, after
kissing her on the forehead, he tells her to knock on the
connecting wall if she needs anything.

"Do your servants know who I am?" she asks.

"I'll tell them in the morning," he says and evidently
does, first thing. The flustered, astonished look on the
housekeeper's face as she's serving breakfast is a look Sylvie recognizes. Familiar territory, a relief in a way. All
night Sylvie spent trying to convince herself that this
unbelievable man, house and turn of events were possible. "He loves me," she kept telling herself. "Dr. John
Wilcox loves me."

After breakfast John takes her into his office and asks
her to drink a bitter-tasting tea to calm her nerves. As
he passes her the cup his hand shakes, and she is very
moved by this and also reassured. He sits beside her on
the sofa and puts his arm around her and says that she
doesn't need to explain about her little legs being female;

he is a doctor after all. Everything else, though, he wants to hear—everything about her.

He prods her with gentle questions, he hazards answers so close to the truth that she senses a holiness in him. Her head drops to his shoulder. She feels exquisitely calm and trusting. Nothing she says seems to surprise or even impress him, not until she mentions her memory spells. "Remarkable," he says, and she feels his body tighten. "Fantastic."

Eventually she falls silent. John strokes her arm and asks, "May I see the legs?" She registers how formal this sounds—"the legs"—as if she carries them in her purse, as if he hasn't heard her calling them Sue. Not that she minds. She is very serene. She lifts her skirt to her waist.

Her eyes are on his face. She is so alert to repulsion that she can detect it in a blink. But his expression is like Mr. Bean's. Absorbed and professional, nothing to do with her.

"May I touch them?" John asks.

She nods.

He crouches down in front of her and starts with the right leg, pressing it as if checking for a break, lightly pinching the skin, asking does she feel this? This? "Yes," she whispers.

"This?"

"Yes."

He taps her knee, and the leg kicks out. He goes on pressing and pinching up to where the white stocking ends, up to the naked thigh and up farther to the little hips in their toddler-sized underwear. She closes her eyes. He immediately lowers her skirt.

They don't talk about her legs again that day. At least, they don't talk about them directly. In order to spend every minute with her, John has cancelled all his appointments. They go for a walk in the park. They hold hands. He tells her he is the only child of deceased parents. His father invented the grip in the bobby pin, that's where the money comes from. After lunch in a ritzy restaurant they wander into a bridal shop and he picks out a tight white wedding gown that he insists on buying. "Surely not," she says, for it takes her a few seconds to remember that, by the time of the wedding, she will be able to wear tight dresses. He laughs at what he thinks is her horror at the price tag. In bed that night she tells herself, "I am going to be a normal," but she can't grasp what being a normal means, other than that she will be able to wear the tight white wedding gown and to sleep on her stomach.

The next day John sees patients until lunchtime, then he has her drink two cups of the nerve-calming tea before they go across the city to visit a renowned specialist in congenital malformations.

"I cannot perform the operation myself," John says. "I am not a surgeon. But I will be assisting. I will be right by your side."

The surgeon explains to Sylvie that she is an autosite-parasite. "You are the autosite," he says. "They"—he gestures at her lap—"are the parasite." He shows her pictures of other autosite-parasites: a boy in a turban who has a headless body growing out of his stomach, and a drawing of a man who has a foot coming out of his mouth. He then has Sylvie remove both pairs of her underpants and lie on a table, her own knees bent and draped with a sheet. John, standing beside the surgeon, tells him that both bowels function normally, both menstrual cycles are regular and not necessarily simultaneous, and that although both vaginas have been penetrated, she is, strictly speaking, still a virgin.

He assured her of her virginity yesterday, after she told him about the boy sticking his finger up her. The surgeon's fingers are in greased, clear-plastic gloves. It must be the tea, Sylvie thinks, wondering at how unabashed she feels. Why isn't she having one of her memory spells? She is so relaxed, in fact, she could sleep. She closes her eyes, and her mind drifts to last night and John kissing her at her bedroom door, a long kiss on the lips that left her little legs tingling.

The surgeon is optimistic that not only will he be able to remove her legs and hips but that he will also succeed in ridding her of what he calls her excess plumbing. Over the next few weeks Sylvie and John go to see him twice more at his office, and then the three of them fly to consult another specialist in New York City. As it happens, the side show is in New Jersey, and after her examination, while John and the doctors are conferring, Sylvie takes a taxi to the fairgrounds.

She cries as she is being hugged and congratulated. She had no idea how homesick she was. Mr. Bean admits to having made the biggest mistake of his life, letting John buy her contract. Half-joking, he tries to talk her out of the operation. "Why would a four-leaf clover want to be an ordinary three-leaf?" he asks.

He's upset because attendance has dropped off. When Sylvie and Merry Mary are alone in their old trailer, Mary says that he had better get used to it, side shows are becoming a thing of the past. "I'm thinking of going on a diet," she says.

"I guess I got out just in time," Sylvie says. She tells Mary about John's library, where she spends her days reading. She describes the tight white wedding gown.

"Boy oh boy, you hit the jackpot," Mary says.

"I love John with all my heart," Sylvie says sincerely.

Mary tugs up her shift to aerate her thighs. The pink mounds of her knees have always struck Sylvie as vulnerable, recalling the bald heads of old men. In her act, Mary informs the audience that each of her thighs has the circumference of a big man's chest. Sylvie thinks with a thrill of John's lean chest, how it would lose out to Mary's thigh. "I'm so happy," she tells Mary.

Mary fans herself with the hem of her skirt. "So, what happens to Sue?" she asks.

"What do you mean?" Sylvie says.

"After the operation. What's the doc going to do with her?"

Sylvie feels light-headed.

"See," Mary says, "why I'm asking is I bought four plots in that cemetery where the baby is. One plot for her, two for me, and they threw in a fourth one half price, so I got one extra. Sue's welcome to it if you need some place."

Mary's huge moon face overlays but does not obscure the face of the surgeon, two weeks ago, listening to her heart and saying, "In Frankfurt I excised an abdominal tumour that turned out to contain teeth, hair and an undeveloped spine."

"Free, of course," Mary adds. "No charge."

Sylvie cannot look at Mary. She looks at her new dia-mond-and-gold watch and is startled by how late it is. "Five o'clock!" she exclaims. The watch in her memory, the one on the surgeon's wrist, says four-thirty, the time she should have left the fairgrounds by. Five minutes later she is on the street, climbing into a taxi.

It's a long drive back to the hotel, the taxi is caught in rush-hour traffic. "Two legs do not add up to a human being," she says to herself. The night before last John said, "Just keep telling yourself that." He said, "There is no Sue."

They were in a restaurant, drinking champagne to celebrate the future her. When she repeated "There is no Sue," he kissed the tips of each of her fingers, then presented her with the diamond-and-gold watch. After-ward, crossing the parking lot, he stopped and pressed her against a wall, pressing his hips against her little legs, and kissed her on the mouth.

On the drive home Sylvie's little legs started to twitch, but after a minute they settled into slow, rhythmic kicks under her skirt. It made her feel languid to hold her lit-tle knees. She and John didn't speak, except once she said, "Oh, look!" at the ovations of fireflies glittering along her side of the road. She thought of the fireflies she had caught and preserved in her first scrapbook—a page of them. Until her mother said, "They have to be alive, stupid," she had turned to that page every night, wondering where the lights were.

John was nervous. He held her hand too tightly as they walked from the car to the door of his house. Sylvie *wasn't* nervous, she didn't know why. She tried to startle herself by thinking, "In a few minutes I will be in his bedroom," but once they were inside the house John didn't take her upstairs, he took her into his office. He threw the cushions off the sofa and pulled it out into a bed. Then he turned to her and began to kiss her on the mouth while undoing her blouse. His hands shook, reminding her of when he gave the tea and also that he was no surgeon. Since there were a lot of buttons (she was wearing a high-necked Victorian blouse), she started undoing some herself. She wanted him to know that she was willing. He started clawing at his own clothes as if they were on fire.

As soon as he was naked he resumed helping her, pulling her stockings over her ankles, yanking down her skirt before it was undone. Popping a button. They still didn't speak. He was out of breath. He drew the combs from her hair and let them drop on the floor.

And then he stopped. On his knees in front of her, his hands on her knees, he stopped.

Sylvie closed her eyes. "Do you call ten dollars a bargain?" her mother shouted. "Sure," her father shrugged, backing away, "bargain." "Ten dollars?" her mother shouted. "Ten dollars?"

"God." That was outside her head, that was John. He yanked down Sue's underpants, pulling off her stockings and shoes at the same time.

A great tremor went through her little legs, which then began to clasp his thighs and kick out, clasp and kick out. The moment of pain was nothing compared to the spectacular relief. Sylvie felt as if her little vagina were a yards-long sucking tube, and he was heading right out the back and into her own vagina. She felt a second sharp pain at what she imagined was the point of entry into her own vagina, and after that she felt him as a lightning rod conducting heat and pleasure from Sue to herself.

When he began to ejaculate, he dug his hands under her hips and lifted her, crushing her little groin into his and bringing on her first orgasm. The waves of the orgasm rolled up his lightning-rod penis into her own vagina and along to her own clitoris, where she had another, more luxurious orgasm.

For a few seconds longer, her little legs went on kicking. He seemed to wait them out. Then he withdrew and rolled onto his back. She ran her hand up and down the goosebumps on her little thigh.

"God," he said. "Oh, Sylvie, God." He sounded stricken.

Her hand stopped moving. "What?" she said.

"We got carried away," he said.

"Yes," she said uncertainly.

"I had no idea," he said.

She waited, frightened.

"Of course," he said, as if hitting upon some comfort, "this presents a whole new angle."

Doors slammed in her mind. He didn't want to marry her. He couldn't let her have the operation, not now, and unless she had the operation, he wouldn't marry her.

"New territory," he said. "New data."

Her feet were cold, sunk in mud at the edge of the duck pond. Her little feet were tucked in the folds of her flannel nightgown. There were crickets.

"But perhaps I'm being presumptuous," he said. He paused. "Tell me, did . . . did what I think happened, happen?"

She turned her head to look at him. "Did what happen?"

He kept his eyes on the ceiling. "Did you experience orgasm with your . . ."

She looked down at his left hand. He was rubbing his thumb and forefinger together so hard, he was making the noise that, for a second, she had thought she was hearing in her memory spell, a noise at the pond. "Two," she said quietly. "I had two, I think. I mean, I know I did."

"Two?"

"One in each place."

He reached for her hand and squeezed it but kept his eyes on the ceiling. After a moment he said, "We can pretend it never happened, you know. You see, technically speaking, you have not had intercourse. By you I mean you the autosite, the host body."

"Nothing has changed," she said, but it was a question.

"No, no," he said. "Not as far as you're concerned."

Back at the hotel, he is waiting for her on the sidewalk. He pays the taxi and takes her up to their room. He is very excited. The amputation (he uses this word for the first time) is set for three weeks today, here in New York. Wonderful, she says. He reaches for her hand and brings it to his lips. He won't deceive her: the first operation isn't entirely without risk, and there will be a long and not altogether comfortable recovery. But the follow-up operations will be less strenuous and will contain almost no risk. When the bandages come off, she is not to be frightened. The scarring will eventually be reduced by plastic surgery.

"I won't be frightened," she promises.

During the next three weeks, whenever she is with him, she has no doubts. But alone at night, in her bedroom, she starts to worry. Her little legs kick and fret. They know, she thinks, horrified. They know. They are licentious. Between her own legs, there is nothing, but between her little legs the urge for him is almost past bearing. She is overcome by terrible memories—her mother burning her scrapbooks, burning the picture of her father's mother in its filigreed frame . . . burns on her father's hands. She doesn't know why, maybe it was Merry Mary's offer of the burial plot, but baby Sue's perfect face keeps appearing to her. Will she forget baby Sue's face? What if her freak memory is connected with her freak legs? What if she becomes somebody else for whom nothing that happened to the person she was will be worth preserving?

The mornings after these nights she can't believe what went through her mind only a few hours before. "You're a candidate for the loony bin," she tells herself. The housekeeper brings in her tea, that bitter tea she's starting to acquire a taste for. John pours it. If he has any misgivings about the operation, he never shows them. He talks about the future. They are going to have four children. They are going to visit her father's village in Portugal.

Two days before the operation they return with the surgeon to New York City. Blood tests have to be done, more X-rays need to be taken, and John and the surgeon are giving a news conference. The surgeon wants Sylvie at the conference, but John is afraid that some of the questions might upset her, so she's not attending, which is fine with her.

As the conference is scheduled for the afternoon of their arrival, John has time only to take her up to her hospital room. After he's gone she lies on her bed and listens to "Vic and Sade" on the radio.

About ten minutes go by, and then a nurse barges into the room and hands her a hospital gown to change into. Throwing open the curtains, the nurse says that Thursday is the big day. She pretends not to be dying of curiosity, but Sylvie isn't fooled and she undresses facing her, letting her catch a glimpse.

Throughout the rest of the afternoon nurses and interns arrive to take blood and her temperature or just to plump her pillow, and cleaners keep coming in to mop the floor and to empty the empty wastepaper basket. Sylvie sits on her bed with her skirt hiked above her little knees. Why not give them a thrill? she thinks wistfully.

Around six o'clock John returns with their dinner on a tray, and they eat at the desk. "The news conference went very, very well," he says. Pushing away his half-eaten meal, he gets up and prowls the room. "This is a very, very important operation in terms of certain precedents," he says. He reminds her of Mr. Bean on opening

night in a big city. Before he leaves for the hotel, he fills
her coffee cup with water and has her take two sleeping
pills.

The next day, Wednesday, it's mostly doctors who
keep coming into her room. They don't have to put
on any acts. They pull up her hospital gown and take
good looks, and if a couple of them arrive at the same
time, they talk with each other about her little womb
and menstrual cycles and bowel movements. Sometimes
they ask her questions, sometimes they don't even say
hello. Off and on John pops in to see how she is. He isn't
as keyed-up as he was the day before, but he has meet-
ings and can't stay for long.

When she is wheeled out on a stretcher to have X-
rays, patients are lined along the corridors, waiting for
her. She feels like a float in a parade. When she returns
to her room, John is at the desk having his dinner, but
there's no meal for her because she isn't allowed to eat
now until after the operation. "Am I allowed sleeping
pills?" she asks anxiously, afraid of what she might start
thinking, and remembering, if she lies awake. John pulls
out a bottle from his coat pocket. "How many do you
think you'll need?" he asks.

A nurse wakes her before dawn to wash her and to
shave the pubic hair from herself and from Sue. Several minutes later John and another nurse and an intern
come in.

"This is it," John says.

He keeps her calm by holding her hand as she is
wheeled down the corridors and into the operating the-
atre. She is brought to the centre of what seems like a

stage. John scans the rows of doctors seated behind glass in the encircling tiers. "There are some big names here," he says quietly.

"John?" she says.

He bends toward her. "Yes?"

She gazes at his beautiful face. She can't remember what she was going to say.

"Are you ready, darling?" he asks.

She nods.

A doctor places the ether mask over her mouth and starts the countdown. Still holding her hand, John leans to look into her eyes. The doctor says nine. John's eyes bore into her. The doctor says eight, seven. Sylvie's eyelids drop.

Light hits glass and magnifies something. A polyphemus moth! she thinks excitedly. The light and the magnification grow stronger and stronger until she realizes that what she is looking at is even more infinitesimal than the moth's atoms.

It resembles a vast pine forest. A needle on one of the trees is magnified and becomes a million exotic fish, then one of the fish's scales is magnified and becomes a galaxy of fireflies.

The magnification stops there. The fireflies are lit. "They must be alive," she thinks, and later, weeks later, John will try to cheer her up by telling her how she said this in a loud voice just before going under, and how it drew a laugh from the doctors seated in the gallery.

PRESBYTERIAN
CROSSWALK

SOMETIMES Beth floated. Two or three feet off the ground, and not for very long, ten seconds or so. She wasn't aware of floating when she was actually doing it, however. She had to land and feel a glowing sensation before she realized that she had just been up in the air.

The first time it happened she was on the church steps. She looked back down the walk and knew that she had floated up it. A couple of days later she floated down the outside cellar stairs of her house. She ran inside and told her grandmother, who whipped out the pen and the little pad she carried in her skirt pocket and drew a circle with a hooked nose.

Beth looked at it. "Has Aunt Cora floated, too?" she asked.

Her grandmother nodded.

"When?"

Her grandmother held up six fingers.

"Six years ago?"

Shaking her head, her grandmother held her hand at thigh level.

"Oh," Beth said, "when she was six."

When Beth was six, five years ago, her mother ran off with a man down the street who wore a toupee that curled up in humid weather. Beth's grandmother, her father's mother, came to live with her and her father. Thirty years before that, Beth's grandmother had had her tonsils taken out by a quack who ripped out her vocal chords and the underside of her tongue.

It was a tragedy, because she and her twin sister, Cora, had been on the verge of stardom (or so Cora said) as a professional singing team. They had made two long-play records: "The Carlisle Sisters, Sea to Sea" and "Christmas with the Carlisle Sisters." Beth's grandmother liked to play the records at high volume and to mouth the words. "My prairie home is beautiful, but oh . . ." If Beth sang along, her grandmother might stand next to her and sway and swish her skirt as though Beth were Cora and the two of them were back on stage.

The cover of the "Sea to Sea" album had a photograph of Beth's grandmother and Aunt Cora wearing middies and sailor hats and shielding their eyes with one hand as they peered off in different directions. Their hair, blond and billowing out from under their hats, was glamorous, but Beth secretly felt that even if her grandmother hadn't lost her voice she and Cora would never have been big stars because they had hooked noses, what Cora called Roman noses. Beth was relieved that she hadn't inherited their noses, although she regretted not having got their soft, wavy hair, which they both still wore long, in a braid or falling in silvery drifts down their backs. Beth's grandmother still put on blue eye shadow and red lipstick, too, every morning. And around the house she wore her old, flashy, full-length stage skirts, faded now—red, orange or yellow, or flowered, or with swirls of broken-off sequins. Beth's grandmother didn't care about sloppiness or dirt. With the important exception of Beth's father's den, the house was a mess —Beth was just beginning to realize and be faintly ashamed of this.

On each of Beth's grandmother's skirts was a sewed-on pocket for her pencil and pad. Due to arthritis in her thumb she held the pencil between her middle finger and forefinger, but she still drew faster than anyone Beth had ever seen. She always drew people instead of writing out their name or their initials. Beth, for instance, was a circle with tight, curly hair. Beth's friend Amy was an exclamation mark. If the phone rang and nobody was home, her grandmother answered it and tapped her pencil three times on the receiver to let whoever was on the other end know that it was her and that they should leave a message. "Call," she would write, and then do a drawing.

A drawing of a man's hat was Beth's father. He was a hard-working lawyer who stayed late at the office. Beth had a hazy memory of him giving her a bath once, it must have been before her mother ran off. The memory embarrassed her. She wondered if he wished that she had gone with her mother, if, in fact, she was supposed to have gone, because when he came home from work and she was still there, he seemed surprised. "Who do we have here?" he might say. He wanted peace and quiet. When Beth got rambunctious, he narrowed his eyes as though she gave off a bright, painful light.

Beth knew that he still loved her mother. In the top drawer of his dresser, in an old wallet he never used, he had a snapshot of her mother wearing only a black slip. Beth remembered that slip, and her mother's tight black dress with the zipper down the back. And her long red fingernails that she clicked on tables. "Your mother was too young to marry," was her father's sole disclosure. Her grandmother disclosed nothing, pretending to be deaf if Beth asked about her mother. Beth remembered how her mother used to phone her father for money and how, if her grandmother answered and took the message, she would draw a big dollar sign and then an upside-down v sitting in the middle of a line—a witch's hat.

A drawing of an upside-down v without a line was church. When a Presbyterian church was built within walking distance, Beth and her grandmother started going to it, and her grandmother began reading the Bible and counselling Beth by way of biblical quotations. A few months later a crosswalk appeared at the end of the street, and for several years Beth thought that it was a "Presbyterian" instead of a "Pedestrian" crosswalk and that the sign above it said Watch for Presbyterians.

Her Sunday school teacher was an old, teary-eyed woman who started every class by singing "When Mothers of Salem," while the children hung up their coats and sat down cross-legged on the floor in front of her. That hymn, specifically the part about Jesus wanting to hold children to His "bosom," made Beth feel that there was something not right about Jesus, and consequently it was responsible for her six months of anxiety that she would end up in hell. Every night, after saying her prayers, she would spend a few minutes chanting, "I love Jesus, I love Jesus, I love Jesus," the idea being

that she could talk herself into it. She didn't expect to
feel earthly love; she awaited the unknown feeling called
glory.

When she began to float, she said to herself, "This is
glory."

She floated once, sometimes twice a week. Around
Christmas it began to happen less often—every ten days
to two weeks. Then it dwindled down to only about
once a month. She started to chant "I love Jesus" again,
not because she was worried any more about going to
hell, she just wanted to float.

By the beginning of the summer holidays she hadn't
floated in almost seven weeks. She phoned her Aunt
Cora who said that, yes, floating was glory all right, but
that Beth should consider herself lucky it had happened
even once. "Nothing that good lasts long," she sighed.
Beth couldn't stop hoping, though. She went to the
park and climbed a tree. Her plan was to jump and have
Jesus float her to the ground. But as she stood on a limb,
working up her courage, she remembered God seeing
the little sparrow fall and letting it fall anyway, and she
climbed down.

She felt that she had just had a close call. She lay on
her back on the picnic table, gazing up in wonder at how
high up she had been. It was a hot, still day. She heard
heat bugs and an ambulance. Presently she went over to
the swings and took a turn on each one, since there was
nobody else in the park.

She was on the last swing when Helen McCormack came waddling across the lawn, calling that a boy had just been run over by a car. Beth slid off the swing. "He's almost dead!" Helen called.

"Who?" Beth asked.

"I don't know his name. Nobody did. He's about eight. He's got red hair. The car ran over his leg *and* his back."

"Where?"

Helen was panting. "I shouldn't have walked so fast," she said, holding her hands on either side of her enormous head. "My cranium veins are throbbing." Little spikes of her wispy blond hair stood out between her fingers.

"Where did it happen?" Beth said.

"On Glenmore. In front of the post office."

Beth started running toward Glenmore, but Helen called, "There's nothing there now, everything's gone!" so Beth stopped and turned, and for a moment Helen and the swings seemed to continue turning, coming round and round like Helen's voice saying, "You missed the whole thing. You missed it. You missed the whole thing."

"He was on his bike," Helen said, dropping onto a swing, "and an eyewitness said that the car skidded on water and knocked him down, then ran over him twice, once with a front tire and once with a back one. I got there before the ambulance. He probably won't live. You could tell by his eyes. His eyes were glazed." Helen's eyes, blue, huge because of her glasses, didn't blink.

"That's awful," Beth said.

"Yes, it really was," Helen said, matter-of-factly. "He's not the first person I've seen who nearly died, though. My aunt nearly drowned in the bathtub when we were staying at her house. She became a human vegetable."

"Was the boy bleeding?" Beth asked.

"Yes, there was blood everywhere."

Beth covered her mouth with both hands.

Helen looked thoughtful. "I think he'll probably die," she said. She pumped her fat legs but without enough energy to get the swing going. "I'm going to die soon," she said.

"You are?"

"You probably know that I have water on the brain," Helen said.

"Yes, I know that," Beth said. Everyone knew. It was why Helen wasn't supposed to run. It was why her head was so big.

"Well, more and more water keeps dripping in all the time, and one day there will so much that my brain will literally drown in it."

"Who said?"

"The doctors, who else?"

"They said, 'You're going to die'?"

Helen threw her an ironic look. "Not exactly. What they tell you is, you're not going to live." She squinted up at a plane going by. "The boy, he had . . . I think it was a rib, sticking out of his back."

"Really?"

"I *think* it was a rib. It was hard to tell because of all the blood." With the toe of her shoe, Helen began to jab a hole in the sand under her swing. "A man from the post office hosed the blood down the sewer, but some of it was already caked from the sun."

Beth walked toward the shade of the picnic table. The air was so thick and still. Her arms and legs, cutting through it, seemed to produce a thousand soft clashes.

"The driver was an old man," Helen said, "and he was crying uncontrollably."

"Anybody *would* cry," Beth said hotly. Her eyes filled with tears.

Helen squirmed off her swing and came over to the table. Grunting with effort, she climbed onto the seat across from Beth and began to roll her head. "At least *I'll* die in one piece," she said.

"Are you really going to?" Beth asked.

"Yep." Helen rotated her head three times one way, then three times the other. Then she propped it up with her hands cupped under her chin.

"But can't they do anything to stop the water dripping in?" Beth asked.

"Nope," Helen said distantly, as if she were thinking about something more interesting.

"You know what?" Beth said, swiping at her tears. "If every night, you closed your eyes and chanted over and over, 'Water go away, water go away, water go away,' maybe it would start to, and then your head would shrink down."

Helen smirked. "Somehow," she said, "I doubt it."

From the edge of the picnic table Beth tore a long sliver of wood like the boy's rib. She pictured the boy riding his bike no-hands, zigzagging down the street the way boys did. She imagined bursting Helen's head with the splinter to let the water gush out.

"I'm thirsty," Helen sighed. "I've had a big shock today. I'm going home for some lemonade."

Beth went with her. It was like walking with her grandmother, who, because of arthritis in her hips, also rocked from side to side and took up the whole sidewalk. Beth asked Helen where she lived.

"I can't talk," Helen panted. "I'm trying to breathe."

Beth thought that Helen lived in the apartments where the immigrants, crazy people and bums were, but Helen went past those apartments and up the hill to the new Regal Heights subdivision, which had once been a landfill site. Her house was a split-level with a little turret above the garage. On the door was an engraved wooden sign, the kind that Beth had seen nailed to posts in front of cottages. No Solicitors, it said.

"My father is a solicitor," Beth said.

Helen was concentrating on opening the door. "Darn thing's always stuck," she muttered as she shoved it open with her shoulder. "I'm home!" she hollered, then sat heavily on a small mauve suitcase next to the door.

Across the hallway a beautiful woman was dusting the ceiling with a mop. She had dark, curly hair tied up in a red ribbon, and long, slim legs in white short shorts.

To Beth's amazement she was Helen's mother. "You can call me Joyce," she said, smiling at Beth as though she loved her. "Who's this lump of potatoes," she laughed, pointing the mop at Helen.

Helen stood up. "A boy got run over on Glenmore," she said.

Joyce's eyes widened, and she looked at Beth.

"I didn't see it," Beth told her.

"We're dying of thirst," Helen said. "We want lemonade in my room."

While Joyce made lemonade from a can, Helen sat at the kitchen table, resting her head on her folded arms. Joyce's questions about the accident seemed to bore her. "We don't need ice," she said impatiently when Joyce went to open the freezer. She demanded cookies, and Joyce poured some Oreos onto the tray with their coffee mugs of lemonade, then handed the tray to Beth, saying with a little laugh that, sure as shooting, Helen would tip it over.

"I'm always spilling things," Helen agreed.

Beth carried the tray through the kitchen to the hallway. "Why is that there?" she asked, nodding at the suitcase beside the front door.

"That's my hospital suitcase," Helen said. "It's all packed for an emergency." She pushed open her bedroom door so that it banged against the wall. The walls were the same mauve as the suitcase, and there was a smell of paint. Everything was put away—no clothes lying around, no games or toys on the floor. The dolls and books, lined up on white bookshelves, looked as if they were for sale. Beth thought contritely of her own dolls, their tangled hair and dirty dresses, half of them naked, some of them missing legs and hands, she could never remember why, she could never figure out how a hand got in with her Scrabble letters.

She set the tray down on Helen's desk. Above the desk was a chart that said "Heart Rate," "Blood Pressure" and "Bowel Movements" down the side. "What's that?" she asked.

"My bodily functions chart." Helen grabbed a handful of cookies. "We're keeping track every week to see how much things change before they completely stop. We're conducting an experiment."

Beth stared at the neatly stencilled numbers and the gently waving red lines. She had the feeling that she was missing something as stunning and obvious as the fact that her mother was gone for good. For years after her mother left she asked her father, "When is she coming back?" Her father, looking confused, always answered, "Never," but Beth just couldn't understand what he meant by that, not until she finally thought to ask, "When is she coming back for the rest of her life?"

She turned to Helen. "When are you going to die?"

Helen shrugged. "There's no exact date," she said with her mouth full.

"Aren't you afraid?"

"Why should I be? Dying the way I'm going to doesn't hurt, you know."

Beth sat on the bed. There was the hard feel of plastic under the spread and blankets. She recognized it from when she'd had her tonsils out and they'd put plastic under her sheets then. "I hope that boy hasn't died," she said, suddenly thinking of him again.

"He probably has," Helen said, running a finger along the lowest line in the chart.

The lines were one above the other, not intersecting. When Beth's grandmother drew one wavy line, that was water. Beth closed her eyes. Water go away, she said to herself. Water go away, water go away . . .

"What are you doing?" The bed bounced, splashing lemonade out of Beth's mug as Helen sat down.

"I was conducting an experiment," Beth said.

"What experiment?"

More lemonade, this time from Helen's mug, poured onto Beth's leg and her shorts. "Look what you're doing!" Beth cried. She used the corner of the bedspread to dry herself. "You're so stupid sometimes," she muttered.

Helen drank down what was left in her mug. "For your information," she said, wiping her mouth on her arm, "it's not stupidity. It's deterioration of the part of my brain lobe that tells my muscles what to do."

Beth looked up at her. "Oh, from the water," she said softly.

"Water is one of the most destructive forces known to mankind," Helen said.

"I'm sorry," Beth murmured. "I didn't mean it."

"So what did you mean you were conducting an experiment?" Helen asked, pushing her glasses up on her nose.

"You know what?" Beth said. "We could both do it." She felt a thrill of virtuous resolve. "Remember what I said about chanting 'water go away, water go away'? We could both chant it and see what happens."

"Brother," Helen sighed.

Beth put her lemonade on the table and jumped off the bed. "We'll make a chart," she said, fishing around in the drawer of Helen's desk for a pen and some paper. She found a red pencil. "Do you have any paper?" she asked. "We need paper and a measuring tape."

"Brother," Helen said again, but she left the room and came back a few minutes later with a pad of foolscap and her mother's sewing basket.

Beth wrote "Date" and "Size" at the top of the page and underlined it twice. Under "Date" she wrote "June 30," then she unwound the measuring tape and measured Helen's head—the circumference above her eyebrows—and wrote "27½." Then she and Helen sat cross-legged on the floor, closed their eyes, held each other's hands and said, "Water go away," starting out in almost a whisper, but Helen kept speeding up, and Beth had to raise her voice to slow her down. After a few moments both of them were shouting, and Helen was digging her nails into Beth's fingers.

"Stop!" Beth cried. She yanked her hands free. "It's supposed to be slow and quiet!" she cried. "Like praying!"

"We don't go to church," Helen said, pressing her hands on either side of her head. "Whew," she breathed. "For a minute there I thought that my cranium veins were throbbing again."

"We did it wrong," Beth said crossly. Helen leaned over to get the measuring tape. "You should chant tonight before you go to bed," Beth said, watching as Helen pulled on the bedpost to hoist herself to her feet. "Chant slowly and softly. I'll come back tomorrow after lunch and we'll do it together again. We'll just keep doing it every afternoon for the whole summer, if that's what it takes. Okay?"

Helen was measuring her hips, her wide, womanly hips in their dark green Bermuda shorts.

"*Okay?*" Beth repeated.

Helen bent over to read the tape. "Sure," she said indifferently.

When Beth got back to her own place, her grandmother was playing her "Sea to Sea" record and making black bean soup and dinner rolls. Talking loudly to be heard over the music, Beth told her about the car accident and Helen. Her grandmother knew about Helen's condition but thought that she was retarded—in the flour sprinkled on the table she traced a circle with a triangle sitting on it, which was "dunce," and a question mark.

"No," Beth said, surprised. "She gets all A's."

Her grandmother pulled out her pad and pencil and wrote, "Don't get her hopes up."

"But when you *pray*, that's getting your hopes up," Beth argued.

Her grandmother looked impressed. "We walk by faith," she wrote.

There was a sudden silence. "Do you want to hear side two?" Beth asked. Her grandmother made a cross with her fingers. "Oh, okay," Beth said and went into the living room and put on her grandmother's other record, the Christmas one. The first song was "Hark! the Herald Angels Sing." Beth's father's name was Harold. The black bean soup, his favourite, meant he'd be home for supper. Beth wandered down the hall to his den and sat in his green leather chair and swivelled for a moment to the music. "Offspring of a Virgin's womb . . ."

After a few minutes she got off the chair and began searching through his wastepaper basket. Whenever she was in here and noticed that the basket hadn't been emptied, she looked at what was in it. Usually just pencil shavings and long handwritten business letters with lots of crossed-out sentences and notes in the margins. Sometimes there were phone messages from his office, where he was called Hal, by Sue, the woman who wrote the messages out.

"PDQ!" Sue wrote. "ASAP!"

Today there were several envelopes addressed to her father, a couple of flyers, an empty cigarette package, and a crumpled pink note from her grandmother's pad. Beth opened the note up.

"Call," it said, and then there was an upside-down v. Underneath that was a telephone number.

Beth thought it was a message for her father to call the church. Her mother hadn't called in over four years, so it took a moment of wondering why the phone number didn't start with two fives like every other phone number in the neighbourhood did, and why her father, who didn't go to church, should get a message from the church, before Beth remembered that an upside-down v meant not "church" but "witch's hat."

In the kitchen Beth's grandmother was shaking the bean jars to "Here We Come a-Wassailing." Beth felt the rhythm as a pounding between her ears. "My cranium veins are throbbing," she thought in revelation, and putting down the message she pressed her palms to her temples and remembered when her mother used to phone for money. Because of those phone calls Beth had always pictured her mother and the man with the toupee living in some poor place, a rundown apartment, or one of the insulbrick bungalows north of the city. "I'll bet they're broke again," Beth told herself, working up scorn. "I'll bet they're down to their last penny." She picked up the message and crumpled it back into a ball, then opened it up again, folded it in half and slipped it into the pocket of her shorts.

Sticking to her promise, she went over to Helen's every afternoon. It took her twenty minutes, a little longer than that if she left the road to go through the park, which she often did out of a superstitious feeling that the next time she floated, it would be there. The park made her think of the boy who was run over. On the radio it said that his foot had been amputated and that he was in desperate need of a liver transplant. "Remember him in your prayers," the announcer said, and Beth and her grandmother did. The boy's name was Kevin Legg.

"Kevin *Legg* and he lost his *foot!*" Beth pointed out to Joyce.

Joyce laughed, although Beth hadn't meant it as a joke. A few minutes later, in the bedroom, Beth asked Helen, "Why isn't your mother worried about us getting your hopes up?"

"She's just glad that I finally have a friend," Helen answered. "When I'm by myself, I get in the way of her cleaning."

Beth looked out the window. It hadn't occurred to her that she and Helen were friends.

Beth's best friend, Christine, was at a cottage for the summer. Amy, her other friend, she played with in the mornings and when she returned from Helen's. Amy was half Chinese, small and thin. She was on pills for hyper-activity. "Just think what I'd be like if I *wasn't* on them!" she cried, spinning around and slamming into the wall. Amy was the friend that Beth's grandmother represented with an exclamation mark. Whatever they were playing, Amy got tired of after five minutes, but she usually had another idea. She was fun, although not very nice. When Beth told her about Helen dying, she cried, "That's a lie!"

"Ask her mother," Beth said.

"No way I'm going to that fat-head's place!" Amy cried.

Amy didn't believe the story about the doctor ripping out Beth's grandmother's tonsils, either, not even after Beth's grandmother opened her mouth and showed her her mutilated tongue.

So Beth knew better than to confide in Amy about floating. She knew better than to confide in anybody, aside from her grandmother and her Aunt Cora, since it wasn't something she could prove and since she found it hard to believe herself. At the same time she was pas-sionately certain that she had floated, and might again if she kept up her nightly "I love Jesus" chants.

She confided in Helen about floating, though, on the fifteenth day of *their* chanting, because that day, instead of sitting on the floor and holding Beth's hands, Helen curled up on her side facing the wall and said, "I wish we were playing checkers," and Beth thought how trusting Helen had been so far, chanting twice a day without any reason to believe that it worked.

The next day, the sixteenth day, Helen's head meas-ured twenty-seven inches.

"Are you sure you aren't pulling the tape tighter?" Helen asked.

"No," Beth said. "I always pull it this tight."

Helen pushed the tape off her head and waddled to the bedroom door. "Twenty-seven inches!" she called.

"Let's go show her," Beth said, and they hurried to the living room, where Joyce was using a nail to clean between the floorboards.

"Aren't you guys smart!" Joyce said, sitting back on her heels and wiping specks of dirt from her slim legs and little pink shorts.

"Come on," Helen said, tugging Beth back to the bedroom.

Breathlessly she went to the desk and wrote the measurement on the chart.

Beth sat on the bed. "I can't believe it," she said, falling onto her back. "It's working. I mean I *thought* it would, I *hoped* it would, but I wasn't absolutely, positively, one hundred per cent sure."

Helen sat beside her and began to roll her head. Beth pictured the water sloshing from side to side. "Why do you do that?" she asked.

"I get neck cramps," Helen said. "One thing I won't miss are these darn neck cramps."

The next day her head lost another half inch. The day after that it lost an entire inch, so that it was now down to twenty-five and a half inches. Beth and Helen demonstrated the measurements to Joyce, who acted amazed, but Beth could tell that for some reason she really wasn't.

"We're not making it up," Beth told her.

"Well, who said you were?" Joyce asked, pretending to be insulted.

"Don't you think her head *looks* smaller?" Beth said, and both she and Joyce considered Helen's head, which *had* looked smaller in the bedroom, but now Beth wasn't so sure. In fact, she was impressed, the way she used to be when she saw Helen only once in a while, by just how big Helen's head was. And by her lumpy, grown-up woman's body, which at this moment was collapsing onto a kitchen chair.

"You know, I think maybe it *does* look smaller," Joyce said brightly.

"Wait'll Dr. Dobbs sees me," Helen said in a tired voice, folding her arms on the table and laying her head down.

Joyce gave Helen's shoulder a little punch. "You all right, kiddo?"

Helen ignored her. "I'll show him our chart," she said to Beth.

"Hey," Joyce said. "You all right?"

Helen closed her eyes. "I need a nap," she murmured.

When Beth returned home there was another message from her mother in her father's wastepaper basket.

This time, before she could help herself, she thought, "She wants to come back, she's left that man," and she instantly believed it with righteous certainty. "I *told* you," she said out loud, addressing her father. Her eyes burned with righteousness. She threw the message back in the wastepaper basket and went out to the back yard, where her grandmother was tying up the tomato plants. Her grandmother had on her red blouse with the short, puffy sleeves and her blue skirt that was splattered with what had once been red music notes but which were now faded and broken pink sticks. Her braid was wrapped around her head. "She looks like an immigrant," Beth thought coldly, comparing her to Joyce. For several moments Beth stood there looking at her grandmother and feeling entitled to a few answers.

The instant her grandmother glanced up, however, she didn't want to know. If, right at that moment, her grandmother had decided to tell her what the messages were about, Beth would have run away. As it was, she ran around to the front of the house and down the street. "I love Jesus, I love Jesus," she said, holding her arms out. She was so light on her feet! Any day now she was going to float, she could feel it.

Her father came home early that evening. It seemed significant to Beth that he did not change into casual pants and a sports shirt before supper, as he normally did. Other than that, however, nothing out of the ordinary happened. Her father talked about work, her grandmother nodded and signalled and wrote out a few conversational notes, which Beth leaned over to read.

After supper her father got around to changing his clothes, then went outside to cut the grass while Beth and her grandmother did the dishes. Beth, carrying too many dishes to the sink, dropped and smashed a saucer and a dinner plate. Her grandmother waved her

hands—"Don't worry, it doesn't matter!"—and to prove
it she got the Sears catalogue out of the cupboard and
showed Beth the new set of dinnerware she intended to
buy anyway.

It wasn't until Beth was eating breakfast the next
morning that it dawned on her that if her mother was
coming back, her grandmother would be leaving, and
if her grandmother was leaving, she wouldn't be buying new dinnerware. This thought left Beth feeling as if
she had just woken up with no idea yet what day it was
or what she'd just been dreaming. Then the radio blared
". . . Liver . . ." and she jumped and turned to see her
grandmother with one hand on the volume knob, and
the other hand held up for silence. "Doctors report that
the transplant was a success," the announcer said, "and
that Kevin is in serious but stable condition."

"Did they find a donor?" Beth cried as the announcer
said, "The donor, an eleven-year-old girl, died in St. Andrew's hospital late last night. Her name is being with-
held at her family's request."

Her grandmother turned the volume back down.

"Gee, that's great," Beth said. "Everybody was praying for him."

Her grandmother tore a note off her pad. "Ask and it
shall be given you," she wrote.

"I know!" Beth said exultantly. "I know!"

Nobody was home at Helen's that afternoon. Peer-
ing in the window beside the door, Beth saw that the
mauve suitcase was gone, and the next thing she knew,
she floated from Helen's door to the end of her driveway.
Or at least she thought she floated, because she couldn't

remember how she got from the house to the road, but the strange thing was, she didn't have the glowing sensation, the feeling of glory. She drifted home, holding herself as if she were a soap bubble.

At her house there was a note on the kitchen counter: a drawing of an apple, which meant that her grandmother was out grocery shopping. The phone rang, but when Beth said hello, the person hung up. She went into her bedroom, opened the drawer of her bedside table and took out the message with her mother's phone number on it. She returned to the kitchen and dialled. After four rings, an impatient-sounding woman said, "Hello?" Beth said nothing. "Yes, hello?" the woman said. "Who's calling?"

Beth hung up. She dialled Helen's number and immediately hung up.

She stood there for a few minutes, biting her knuckles.

She wandered down to her bedroom and looked out the window. Two back yards away, Amy was jumping off her porch. She was climbing onto the porch railing, leaping like a broad jumper, tumbling on the grass, springing to her feet, running up the stairs and doing it again. It made Beth's head spin.

About a quarter of an hour later her grandmother returned. She dropped the groceries against a cupboard door that slammed shut. She opened and shut the fridge. Turned on the tap. Beth, now lying on the bed, didn't move. She sat bolt upright when the phone rang, though. Five rings before her grandmother answered it.

Beth got up and went over to the window again. Amy

was throwing a ball up into the air. Through the closed window Beth couldn't hear a thing, but she knew from the way Amy clapped and twirled her hands between catches that she was singing, "Ordinary moving, laughing, talking . . ."

She knew from hearing the chair scrape that her grandmother was pulling it back to sit down. She knew from hearing the faucet still run that her grandmother was caught up in what the caller was saying. Several times her grandmother tapped her pencil on the mouthpiece to say to the caller, "I'm still listening. I'm taking it all down."

NINETY-THREE
MILLION MILES
AWAY

AT LEAST PART of the reason why Ali married Claude, a cosmetic surgeon with a growing practice, was so that she could quit her boring government job. Claude was all for it. "You only have one life to live," he said. "You only have one kick at the can." He gave her a generous allowance and told her to do what she wanted.

She wasn't sure what that was, aside from trying on clothes in expensive stores. Claude suggested something musical—she loved music—so she took dance classes and piano lessons and discovered that she had a tin ear and no sense of rhythm. She fell into a mild depression during which she peevishly questioned Claude about the ethics of cosmetic surgery.

"It all depends on what light you're looking at it in," Claude said. He was not easily riled. What Ali needed to do, he said, was take the wider view.

She agreed. She decided to devote herself to learning, and she began a regimen of reading and studying, five days a week, five to six hours a day. She read novels, plays, biographies, essays, magazine articles, almanacs, the New Testament, *The Concise Oxford Dictionary, The Harper Anthology of Poetry.*

But after a year of this, although she became known as the person at dinner parties who could supply the name or date that somebody was snapping around for, she wasn't particularly happy, and she didn't even feel smart. Far from it, she felt stupid, a machine, an idiot savant whose one talent was memorization. If she had any *creative* talent, which was the only kind she really admired, she wasn't going to find it by armouring herself with facts. She grew slightly paranoid that Claude wanted her to settle down and have a baby.

On their second wedding anniversary they bought a condominium apartment with floor-to-ceiling windows, and Ali decided to abandon her reading regimen and to take up painting. Since she didn't know the first thing about painting or even drawing, she studied pictures from art books. She did know what her first subject was going to be—herself in the nude. A few months ago she'd had a dream about spotting her signature in the corner of a painting, and realizing from the conversation of the men who were admiring it (and blocking her view) that it was an extraordinary rendition of her naked self. She took the dream to be a sign. For two weeks she studied the proportions, skin tones and muscle definitions of the nudes in her books, then she went out and bought art supplies and a self-standing, full-length mirror.

She set up her work area halfway down the living room. Here she had light without being directly in front of the window. When she was all ready to begin, she stood before the mirror and slipped off her white terry-cloth housecoat and her pink flannelette pyjamas, letting them fall to the floor. It aroused her a little to witness her careless shedding of clothes. She tried a pose: hands folded and resting loosely under her stomach, feet buried in the drift of her housecoat.

For some reason, however, she couldn't get a fix on what she looked like. Her face and body seemed indistinct, secretive in a way, as if they were actually well defined, but not to her, or not from where she was looking.

She decided that she should simply start, and see what happened. She did a pencil drawing of herself sitting in a chair and stretching. It struck her as being very good, not that she could really judge, but the out-of-kilter proportions seemed slyly deliberate, and there was a pleasing simplicity to the reaching arms and the elongated curve of the neck. Because flattery hadn't been her intention, Ali felt that at last she may have wrenched a vision out of her soul.

The next morning she got out of bed unusually early, not long after Claude had left the apartment, and discovered sunlight streaming obliquely into the living room through a gap between their building and the apartment house next door. As far as she knew, and in spite of the plate-glass windows, this was the only direct light they got. Deciding to make use of it while it lasted, she moved her easel, chair and mirror closer to the window. Then she took off her housecoat and pyjamas.

For a few moments she stood there looking at herself, wondering what it was that had inspired the sketch. Today she was disposed to seeing herself as not bad, overall. As far as certain specifics went, though, as to whether her breasts were small, for instance, or her eyes close together, she remained in the dark.

Did other people find her looks ambiguous? Claude was always calling her beautiful, except that the way he put it—"You're beautiful to me," or "I think you're beautiful"—made it sound as if she should understand that his taste in women was unconventional. Her only boyfriend before Claude, a guy called Roger, told her she was great but never said how exactly. When they had sex, Roger liked to hold the base of his penis and watch it going in and out of her. Once, he said that there were days he got so horny at the office, his pencil turned him on. (She felt it should have been his pencil sharpener.)

Maybe she was one of those people who are more attractive when they're animated, she thought. She gave it a try. She smiled and tossed her head, she tucked her hair behind her ears. She covered her breasts with her hands. Down her cleavage a drop of sweat slid haltingly, a sensation like the tip of a tongue. She circled her palms until her nipples hardened. She imagined a man's hands . . . not Claude's—a man's hands not attached to any particular man. She looked out the window.

In the apartment across from her she saw a man.

She leapt to one side, behind the drapes. Her heart pounded violently, as if something had thundered by. She stood there hugging herself. The drapes smelled bitter, cabbagey. Her right hand cupped her left breast, which felt like her heart because her pulse was in it.

After a moment she realized that she had started circling both of her palms on her nipples again. She stopped, astonished, then went on doing it but with the same skeptical thrill she used to get when she knew it wasn't *her* moving the ouija board. And then it was her feet that were moving involuntarily, taking her from behind the drapes into a preternatural brightness.

She went to the easel, picked up a brush and the palette and began to mix a skin colour. She didn't look at the window or at the mirror. She had the tranced sensation of being at the edge of a cliff. Her first strokes dripped, so she switched to dabbing at the canvass, producing what started to resemble feathers. Paint splashed on her own skin but she ignored it and went on dabbing, layer on layer until she lost the direct sun. Then she wet a rag in the turpentine and wiped her hands and her breasts and stomach.

She thought about the sun. That it is ninety-three million miles away and that its fuel supply will last another five billion years. Instead of thinking about the man who was watching her, she tried to recall a solar chart she had memorized a couple of years ago.

The surface temperature is six thousand degrees Fahrenheit, she told herself. Double that number and you have how many times bigger the surface of the sun is compared to the surface of the earth. Except that because the sun is a ball of hot gas, it actually has no surface.

When she had rubbed the paint off, she went into the kitchen to wash away the turpentine with soap and water. The man's eyes tracked her. She didn't have to glance at the window for confirmation. She switched on the light above the sink, soaped the dishcloth and began to wipe her skin. There was no reason to clean her arms, but she lifted each one and wiped the cloth over it. She wiped her breasts. She seemed to share in his scrutiny, as if she were looking at herself through his eyes. From his perspective she was able to see her physical self very clearly—her shiny, red-highlighted hair, her small waist and heart-shaped bottom, the dreamy tilt to her head.

She began to shiver. She wrung out the cloth and folded it over the faucet, then patted herself dry with a dish towel. Then, pretending to be examining her fingernails, she turned and walked over to the window. She looked up.

There he was, in the window straight across but one floor higher. Her glance of a quarter of an hour ago had registered dark hair and a white shirt. Now she saw a long, older face, a man in his fifties maybe. A green tie. She had seen him before this morning—quick, disinterested (or so she had thought) sightings of a man in his kitchen, watching television, going from room to room. A bachelor living next door. She pressed the palms of her hands on the window, and he stepped back into shadow.

The pane clouded from her breath. She leaned her body into it, flattening her breasts against the cool glass. Right at the window she was visible to his apartment and the one below, which had closed vertical blinds. "Each window like a pill'ry appears," she thought. Vaguely appropriate lines from the poems she had read last year were always occurring to her. She felt that he was still watching, but she yearned for proof.

When it became evident that he wasn't going to show himself, she went into the bedroom. The bedroom windows didn't face the apartment house, but she closed them anyway, then got into bed under the covers. Between her legs there was such a tender throbbing that she had to push a pillow into her crotch. Sex addicts must feel like this, she thought. Rapists, child molesters.

She said to herself, "You are a certifiable exhibitionist." She let out an amazed, almost exultant laugh, but instantly fell into a darker amazement as it dawned on her that she really was, she really was an exhibitionist. And what's more, she had been one for years, or at least she had been working up to being one for years.

Why, for instance, did she and Claude live here, in this vulgar low-rise? Wasn't it because of the floor-to-ceiling windows that faced the windows of the house next door?

And what about when she was twelve and became so obsessed with the idea of urinating on people's lawns that one night she crept out of the house after everyone was asleep and did it? Peed on the lawn of the townhouses next door, right under a streetlight, in fact.

What about two years ago, when she didn't wear underpants the entire summer? She'd had a minor yeast infection and had read that it was a good idea not to wear underpants at home, if you could help it, but she had stopped wearing them in public as well, beneath skirts and dresses, at parties, on buses, and she must have known that this was taking it a bit far, because she had kept it from Claude.

"Oh, my God," she said wretchedly.

She went still, alerted by how theatrical that had sounded. Her heart was beating in her throat. She touched a finger to it. So fragile, a throat. She imagined the man being excited by one of her hands circling her throat.

What was going on? What was the matter with her? Maybe she was too aroused to be shocked at herself. She moved her hips, rubbing her crotch against the pillow. No, she didn't want to masturbate. That would ruin it.

Ruin what?

She closed her eyes, and the man appeared to her. She experienced a rush of wild longing. It was as if, all her life, she had been waiting for a long-faced, middle-aged man in a white shirt and green tie. He was probably still standing in his living room, watching her window.

She sat up, threw off the covers.

Dropped back down on the bed.

This was crazy. This really was crazy. What if he was a rapist? What if, right this minute, he was downstairs, finding out her name from the mailbox? Or what if he was just some lonely, normal man who took her display as an invitation to phone her up and ask her for a date? It's not as if she wanted to go out with him. She wasn't looking for an affair.

For an hour or so she fretted, and then she drifted off to sleep. When she woke up, shortly after noon, she was quite calm. The state she had worked herself into earlier struck her as overwrought. So, she gave some guy a thrill, so what? She was a bit of an exhibitionist. Most women were, she bet. It was instinctive, a side effect of being the receptor in the sex act.

She decided to have lunch and go for a walk. While she was making herself a sandwich she avoided glancing at the window, but as soon as she sat at the table she couldn't resist looking over.

He wasn't there, and yet she felt that he was watching her, standing out of the light. She ran a hand through her hair. "For Christ's sake," she reproached herself, but she was already with him. Again it was as if her eyes were in his head, although not replacing his eyes. She knew that he wanted her to slip her hand down her sweat pants. She did this. Watching his window, she removed her hand and licked her wet fingers. At that instant she would have paid money for some sign that he was watching.

After a few minutes she began to chew on her fingernails. She was suddenly depressed. She reached over and pulled the curtain across the window and ate her sandwich. Her mouth, biting into the bread, trembled like an old lady's. "Tremble like a guilty thing surprised," she quoted to herself. It wasn't guilt, though. It wasn't frustration, either, not sexual frustration. She was acquainted with this bleached sadness—it came upon her at the height of sensation. After orgasms, after a day of trying on clothes in stores.

She finished her sandwich and went for a long walk in her new toreador pants and her tight black turtleneck. By the time she returned, Claude was home. He asked her if she had worked in the nude again.

"Of course," she said absently. "I have to." She was looking past him at the man's closed drapes. "Claude," she said suddenly, "am I beautiful? I mean not just to you. Am I empirically beautiful?"

Claude looked surprised. "Well, yeah," he said. "Sure you are. Hell, I married you, didn't I? Hey!" He stepped back. "Whoa!"

She was removing her clothes. When she was naked,

she said, "Don't think of me as your wife. Just as a woman. One of your patients. Am I beautiful or not?"

He made a show of eyeing her up and down. "Not bad," he said. "Of course, it depends what you mean by beautiful." He laughed. "What's going on?"

"I'm serious. You don't think I'm kind of . . . normal? You know, plain?"

"Of course not," he said lovingly. He reached for her and drew her into his arms. "You want hard evidence?" he said.

They went into the bedroom. It was dark because the curtains were still drawn. She switched on the bedside lamp, but once he was undressed he switched it off.

"No," she said from the bed, "leave it on."

"What? You want it on?"

"For a change."

The next morning she got up before he did. She had hardly slept. During breakfast she kept looking over at the apartment house, but there was no sign of the man. Which didn't necessarily mean that he wasn't there. She couldn't wait for Claude to leave so that she could stop pretending she wasn't keyed-up. It was gnawing at her that she had overestimated or somehow misread the man's interest. How did she know? He might be gay. He might be so devoted to a certain woman that all other women repelled him. He might be puritanical, a priest, a Born-Again. He might be out of his mind.

The minute Claude left the apartment, she undressed and began work on the painting. She stood in the sunlight mixing colours, then sat on the chair in her stretching pose, looking at herself in the mirror, then stood up and, without paying much attention, glancing every few seconds at his window, painted ribs and uplifted breasts.

An hour went by before she thought, He's not going to show up. She dropped into the chair, weak with disappointment, even though she knew that, very likely, he had simply been obliged to go to work, that his being home yesterday was a fluke. Forlornly she gazed at her painting. To her surprise she had accomplished something rather interesting: breasts like Picasso eyes. It is possible, she thought dully, that I am a natural talent.

She put her brush in the turpentine, and her face in her hands. She felt the sun on her hair. In a few minutes the sun would disappear behind his house, and after that, if she wanted him to get a good look at her, she would have to stand right at the window. She envisioned herself stationed there all day. You are ridiculous, she told herself. You are unhinged.

She glanced up at the window again.

He was there.

She sat up straight. Slowly she came to her feet. Stay, she prayed. He did. She walked to the window, her fingertips brushing her thighs. She held her breath. When she was at the window, she stood perfectly still. He stood perfectly still. He had on a white shirt again, but no tie. He was close enough that she could make out the darkness around his eyes, although she couldn't tell exactly where he was looking. But his eyes seemed to enter her head like a drug, and she felt herself aligned with his perspective. She saw herself—surprisingly slender, composed but apprehensive—through the glass and against the backdrop of the room's white walls.

After a minute or two she walked to the chair, picked it up and carried it to the window. She sat facing him, her knees apart. He was as still as a picture. So was she, because she had suddenly remembered that he might be gay, or crazy. She tried to give him a hard look. She observed his age and his sad, respectable appearance. And the fact that he remained at the window, revealing his interest.

No, he was the man she had imagined. I am a gift to him, she thought, opening her legs wider. I am his dream come true. She began to rotate her hips. With the fingers of both hands she spread her labia.

One small part of her mind, clinging to the person she had been until yesterday morning, tried to pull her back. She felt it as a presence behind the chair, a tableau of sensational, irrelevant warnings that she was obviously not about to turn around for. She kept her eyes on the man. Moving her left hand up to her breasts, she began to rub and squeeze and to circle her fingers on the nipples. The middle finger of her right hand slipped into her vagina, as the palm massaged her clitoris.

He was motionless.

You are kissing me, she thought. She seemed to feel his lips, cool, soft, sliding and sucking down her stomach. You are kissing me. She imagined his hands under her, lifting her like a bowl to his lips.

She was coming.

Her body jolted. Her legs shook. She had never experienced anything like it. Seeing what he saw, she witnessed an act of shocking vulnerability. It went on and

on. She saw the charity of her display, her lavish reckless-
ness and submission. It inspired her to the tenderest self-
love. The man did not move, not until she had finally
stopped moving, and then he reached up one hand—to
signal, she thought, but it was to close the drapes.

She stayed sprawled in the chair. She was astonished.
She couldn't believe herself. She couldn't believe him.
How did he know to stay so still, to simply watch her?
She avoided the thought that right at this moment he was
probably masturbating. She absorbed herself only with
what she had seen, which was a dead-still man whose eyes
she had sensed roving over her body the way that eyes in
certain portraits seem to follow you around a room.

The next three mornings everything was the same.
He had on his white shirt, she masturbated in the chair,
he watched without moving, she came spectacularly, he
closed the drapes.

Afterwards she went out clothes shopping or visiting people. Everyone told her how great she looked.
At night she was passionate in bed, prompting Claude
to ask several times, "What the hell's come over you?"
but he asked it happily, he didn't look a gift horse in
the mouth. She felt very loving toward Claude, not out
of guilt but out of high spirits. She knew better than
to confess, of course, and yet she didn't believe that she
was betraying him with the man next door. A man who
hadn't touched her or spoken to her, who, as far as she
was concerned, existed only from the waist up and who
never moved except to pull his drapes, how could that
man be counted as a lover?

The fourth day, Friday, the man didn't appear. For

two hours she waited in the chair. Finally she moved to the couch and watched television, keeping one eye on his window. She told herself that he must have had an urgent appointment, or that he had to go to work early. She was worried, though. At some point, late in the afternoon when she wasn't looking, he closed his drapes.

Saturday and Sunday he didn't seem to be home—the drapes were drawn and the lights off. Not that she could have done anything anyway, not with Claude there. On Monday morning she was in her chair, naked, as soon as Claude left the house. She waited until ten-thirty, then put on her toreador pants and white push-up halter-top and went for a walk. A consoling line from *Romeo and Juliet* played in her head: "He that is stricken blind cannot forget the precious treasure of his eyesight lost." She was angry with the man for not being as keen as she was. If he was at his window tomorrow, she vowed she would shut her drapes on him.

But how would she replace him, what would she do? Become a table dancer? She had to laugh. Aside from the fact that she was a respectably married woman and could not dance to save her life and was probably ten years too old, the last thing she wanted was a bunch of slack-jawed, flat-eyed drunks grabbing at her breasts. She wanted one man, and she wanted him to have a sad, intelligent demeanour and the control to watch her without moving a muscle. She wanted him to wear a white shirt.

On the way home, passing his place, she stopped. The building was a mansion turned into luxury apartments. He must have money, she realized. An obvious

conclusion, but until now she'd had no interest whatso-
ever in who he was.

She climbed the stairs and tried the door. Found it
open. Walked in.

The mailboxes were numbered one to four. His
would be four. She read the name in the little window:
Dr. Andrew Halsey.

Back at her apartment she looked him up under "Physicians" in the phone book and found that, like Claude,
he was a surgeon. A general surgeon, though, a remover
of tumours and diseased organs. Presumably on call. Presumably dedicated, as a general surgeon had to be.

She guessed she would forgive his absences.

The next morning and the next, Andrew (as she now
thought of him) was at the window. Thursday he wasn't.
She tried not to be disappointed. She imagined him saving people's lives, drawing his scalpel along skin in beau-
tifully precise cuts. For something to do she worked on
her painting. She painted fish-like eyes, a hooked nose, a
mouth full of teeth. She worked fast.

Andrew was there Friday morning. When Ali saw
him she rose to her feet and pressed her body against the
window, as she had done the first morning. Then she
walked to the chair, turned it around and leaned over it,
her back to him. She masturbated stroking herself from
behind.

That afternoon she bought him a pair of binoculars, an expensive, powerful pair, which she wrapped
in brown paper, addressed and left on the floor in front
of his mailbox. All weekend she was preoccupied with
wondering whether he would understand that she had

given them to him and whether he would use them. She had considered including a message— "For our mornings" or something like that—but such direct communication seemed like a violation of a pact between them. The binoculars alone were a risk.

Monday, before she even had her housecoat off, he walked from the rear of the room to the window, the binoculars at his eyes. Because most of his face was covered by the binoculars and his hands, she had the impression that he was masked. Her legs shook. When she opened her legs and spread her labia, his eyes crawled up her. She masturbated but didn't come and didn't try to, although she put on a show of coming. She was so devoted to his appreciation that her pleasure seemed like a siphoning of his, an early, childish indulgence that she would never return to.

It was later, with Claude, that she came. After supper she pulled him onto the bed. She pretended that he was Andrew, or rather she imagined a dark, long-faced, silent man who made love with his eyes open but who smelled and felt like Claude and whom she loved and trusted as she did Claude. With this hybrid partner she was able to relax enough to encourage the kind of kissing and movement she needed but had never had the confidence to insist upon. The next morning, masturbating for Andrew, she reached the height of ecstasy, as if her orgasms with him had been the fantasy, and her pretences of orgasm were the real thing. Not coming released her completely into his dream of her. The whole show was for him—cunt, ass, mouth, throat offered to his magnified vision.

For several weeks Andrew turned up regularly, five mornings a week, and she lived in a state of elation. In the afternoons she worked on her painting, without much concentration though, since finishing it didn't seem to matter any more in spite of how well it was turning out. Claude insisted that it was still very much a self-portrait, a statement Ali was insulted by, given the woman's obvious primitivism and her flat, distant eyes.

There was no reason for her to continue working in the nude, not in the afternoon, but she did, out of habit and comfort and on the outside chance that Andrew might be home and peeking through his drapes. While she painted she wondered about her exhibitionism, what it was about her that craved to have a strange man look at her. Of course, everyone and everything liked to be looked at to a certain degree, she thought. Flowers, cats, anything that preened or shone, children crying, "Look at me!" Some mornings her episodes with Andrew seemed to have nothing at all to do with lust. They were completely display, wholehearted surrender to what felt like the most inaugural and genuine of all desires, which was not sex but which happened to be expressed through a sexual act.

One night she dreamed that Andrew was operating on her. Above the surgical mask his eyes were expressionless. He had very long arms. She was also able to see, as if through his eyes, the vertical incision that went from between her breasts to her navel, and the skin on either side of the incision folded back like a scroll. Her heart was brilliant red and perfectly heart-shaped. All of her other organs were glistening yellows and oranges.

Somebody should take a picture of this, she thought. Andrew's gloved hands barely appeared to move as they wielded long, silver instruments. There was no blood on his hands. Very carefully, so that she hardly felt it, he prodded her organs and plucked at her veins and tendons, occasionally drawing a tendon out and dropping it into a petri dish. It was as if he were weeding a garden. Her heart throbbed. A tendon encircled her heart, and when he pulled on it she could feel that its other end encircled her vagina, and the uncoiling there was the most exquisite sensation she had ever experienced. She worried that she would come and that her trembling and spasms would cause him to accidentally stab her. She woke up coming.

All day the dream obsessed her. It *could* happen, she reasoned. She could have a gall bladder or an appendicitis attack and be rushed to the hospital and, just as she was going under, see that the surgeon was Andrew. It could happen.

When she woke up the next morning, the dream was her first thought. She looked down at the gentle swell of her stomach and felt sentimental and excited. She found it impossible to shake the dream, even while she was masturbating for Andrew, so that instead of entering *his* dream of her, instead of seeing a naked woman sitting in a pool of morning sun, she saw her sliced-open chest in the shaft of his surgeon's light. Her heart was what she focused on, its fragile pulsing, but she also saw the slower rise and fall of her lungs, and the quivering of her other organs. Between her organs were tantalizing crevices and entwined swirls of blue and red—her veins and arteries. Her tendons were seashell pink, threaded tight as guitar strings.

Of course she realized that she had the physiology all wrong and that in a real operation there would be blood and pain and she would be anaesthetized. It was an impossible, mad fantasy. She didn't expect it to last. But every day it became more enticing as she authenticated it with hard data, such as the name of the hospital he operated out of (she called his number in the phone book and asked his nurse) and the name of the surgical instruments he would use (she consulted one of Claude's medical texts), and as she smoothed out the rough edges by imagining, for instance, minuscule suction tubes planted here and there in the incision to remove every last drop of blood.

In the mornings, during her real encounters with Andrew, she became increasingly frustrated until it was all she could do not to quit in the middle, close the drapes or walk out of the room. And yet if he failed to show up she was desperate. She started to drink gin and tonics before lunch and to sunbathe at the edge of the driveway between her building and his, knowing he wasn't home from ten o'clock on, but lying there for hours, just in case.

One afternoon, light-headed from gin and sun, restless with worry because he hadn't turned up the last three mornings, she changed out of her bikini and into a strapless cotton dress and went for a walk. She walked past the park she had been heading for, past the stores she had thought she might browse in. The sun bore down. Strutting by men who eyed her bare shoulders, she felt voluptuous, sweetly rounded. But at the pit of her stomach was a filament of anxiety, evidence that despite telling herself otherwise, she knew where she was going.

She entered the hospital by the Emergency doors and wandered the corridors for what seemed like half an hour before discovering Andrew's office. By this time she was holding her stomach and half believing that the feeling of anxiety might actually be a symptom of something very serious.

"Dr. Halsey isn't seeing patients," his nurse said. She slit open a manila envelope with a lion's head letter opener. "They'll take care of you at Emergency."

"I have to see Dr. Halsey," Ali said, her voice cracking. "I'm a friend."

The nurse sighed. "Just a minute." She stood and went down a hall, opening a door at the end after a quick knock.

Ali pressed her fists into her stomach. For some reason she no longer felt a thing. She pressed harder. What a miracle if she burst her appendix! She should stab herself with the letter opener. She should at least break her fingers, slam them in a drawer like a draft dodger.

"Would you like to come in?" a high, nasal voice said. Ali spun around. It was Andrew, standing at the door.

"The doctor will see you," the nurse said impatiently, sitting back behind her desk.

Ali's heart began to pound. She felt as if a pair of hands were cupping and uncupping her ears. His shirt was blue. She went down the hall, squeezing past him without looking up, and sat in the chair beside his desk. He shut the door and walked to the window. It was a big room. There was a long expanse of old green and yellow floor tiles between them. Leaning his hip against a filing cabinet, he just stood there, hands in his trouser pockets, regarding her with such a polite, impersonal expression that she asked him if he recognized her.

"Of course I do," he said quietly.

"Well—" Suddenly she was mortified. She felt like a woman about to sob that she couldn't afford the abortion. She touched her fingers to her hot face.

"I don't know your name," he said.

"Oh. Ali. Ali Perrin."

"What do you want, Ali?"

Her eyes fluttered down to his shoes—black, shabby loafers. She hated his adenoidal voice. What did she want? What she wanted was to bolt from the room like the mad woman she suspected she was. She glanced up at him again. Because he was standing with his back to the window, he was outlined in light. It made him seem unreal, like a film image superimposed against a screen. She tried to look away, but his eyes held her. Out in the waiting room the telephone was ringing. What do *you* want, she thought, capitulating to the pull of her perspective over to his, seeing now, from across the room, a charming woman with tanned, bare shoulders and blushing cheeks.

The light blinked on his phone. Both of them glanced at it, but he stayed standing where he was. After a moment she murmured. "I have no idea what I'm doing here."

He was silent. She kept her eyes on the phone, waiting for him to speak. When he didn't, she said, "I had a dream . . ." She let out a disbelieving laugh. "God." She shook her head.

"You are very lovely," he said in a speculative tone. She glanced up at him, and he turned away. Pressing his hands together, he took a few steps along the window. "I have very much enjoyed our . . . our encounters."

"Oh, don't worry," she said. "I'm not here to—"

"However," he cut in, "I should tell you that I am moving into another building."

She looked straight at him.

"This weekend, as a matter of fact." He frowned at his wall of framed diplomas.

"This weekend?" she said.

"Yes."

"So," she murmured. "It's over, then."

"Regrettably."

She stared at his profile. In profile he was a stranger —beak-nosed, round-shouldered. She hated his shoes, his floor, his formal way of speaking, his voice, his profile, and yet her eyes filled and she longed for him to look at her again.

Abruptly he turned his back to her and said that his apartment was in the east end, near the beach. He gestured out the window. Did she know where the yacht club was?

"No," she whispered.

"Not that I am a member," he said with a mild laugh.

"Listen," she said, wiping her eyes. "I'm sorry." She came to her feet. "I guess I just wanted to see you."

He strode like an obliging host over to the door.

"Well, goodbye," she said, looking up into his face.

He had garlic breath and five-o'clock shadow. His eyes grazed hers. "I wouldn't feel too badly about anything," he said affably.

When she got back to the apartment the first thing she did was take her clothes off and go over to the full-length mirror, which was still standing next to the easel. Her eyes filled again because without Andrew's appreciation or the hope of it (and despite how repellant she had found him) what she saw was a pathetic little woman with pasty skin and short legs.

She looked at the painting. If *that* was her, as Claude claimed, then she also had flat eyes and crude, wild proportions.

What on earth did Claude see in her?

What had Andrew seen? "You are very lovely," Andrew had said, but maybe he'd been reminding himself. Maybe he'd meant "lovely when I'm in the next building."

After supper that evening she asked Claude to lie with her on the couch, and the two of them watched TV. She held his hand against her breast. "Let this be enough," she prayed.

But she didn't believe it ever would be. The world was too full of surprises, it frightened her. As Claude was always saying, things looked different from different angles and in different lights. What this meant to her was that everything hinged on where you happened to be standing at a given moment, or even on who you imagined you were. It meant that in certain lights, desire sprang up out of nowhere.

THE
TWO-HEADED
MAN

MY MEMORY is photographic, in living colour. I'm flooded with memories, mostly images from dreams I've had. A leather jacket with four tulips, eating blueberries half blind and having blueberries scattered on the ground, growing limbs that turn out to be tree limbs, useless.

I remember all my nightmares, they come back twice as horrible. My heart stops.

My heart stops at the back of my throat. Anger hits me above my left ear, there's a pressure there, like a finger pushing. Fear is between the eyes. Instead of my guts turning over I feel a popping at the bridge of my nose. After a few seconds the sensation, whatever it is, turns into a burning sensation, a slow smouldering that can last up to five minutes. Sometimes I've got half a dozen of these fires going on at once, all over, overlapping.

What's happening is that my brain messages aren't getting through. My brain works like anybody else's, it sends out messages to the body. But in my case the messages hit a roadblock at Samuel's collarbone. They are all fuelled up for a long trip, and then they have to reverse into my head and park with their engines idling until they burn themselves out.

Inside I'm a mess of burn tissue. Scientists can't wait for me to die so they can open me up and get a good look. Just a couple of days ago a woman researcher wrote me, asking would I donate myself to her lab. I thought of writing back, "Anytime you want me to give you head." I had Samuel write her and ask for an eight-by-ten. If she looks anything like Jill St. John, I'm hers.

An entire week, and not a word from Karen. I suppose I attributed to her a courage she never had. I have always known that I was meant for unhappiness, and yet the human heart yearns. Did not the Son of God yearn? And did He not weep to be forsaken?

It occurs to me that the physical agony Christ suffered on the cross served to distract Him from the more terrible agony of abandonment. God's subtle mercies . . . with which man interferes! I am offered excruciating pain by God, and a painkiller by the nurse. A painkiller! I have thought of saying to her, "If it were that easy, do you think I'd have used a saw?"

My lawyer has warned me about my wry sense of humour. She has urged me to list all the ways Simon persecuted me. So far I've written:

—Biting my ear, provoking numerous chronic infections. Also yelling into that ear, eventually causing deafness.

—Regularly assailing me and everyone around us with the most despicable imprecations.

—Depriving me of sleep. Waking me in the middle of the night with his howling.

—Depriving me of love by tormenting my beloved.

—Libelling me. Telling people that I stuck him with pins, punched him and burned his eyes with Javex.

Nobody believed Simon's lies. If I caused him pain, it was never intentional, our mother having instilled in me a conviction that he was my cross to bear. It was not until our mother died that I understood God's intention was not that I should bear him but that I should cast him off. And even then I thought of "casting off" only in its figurative sense—ridding him of his power to hurt or influence me. At that point I was naive enough, pompous enough, to imagine that I could subdue him. For the first time in our lives I raised my voice at him, and for the first time (in spite of what he claimed) I gagged him in order to compel him to listen.

Sure, Samuel's going to waste me. I've always known that. The question is, how. And when. When is soon, now that the old lady has kicked the bucket. How? I'll tell you one thing, it won't be poison.

Everything I eat or drink, he siphons off. I used to have the old lady spike my coffee. It was hilarious. I'm guzzling gin and coffee, feeling nothing except maybe a nice sweet shimmer, and Samuel's sliding off his chair.

The way I look at it, you've got a brain, you've got all the power you need. Doctors will tell you I can't do fuck all, it's Samuel who's the whole man with the limbs and organs, and I'm nothing but this turd he carries around on his shoulder. But what the doctors don't know, what even Samuel doesn't know, is that I've developed my brain to the point that I'm a master of extrasensory manipulation.

There have been a couple of times I've played Samuel like remote control. One night I was really cooking. He was on his way to a fellowship meeting, and I think, "Hang a left," and suddenly he turns left. I think, "Cross the road," he crosses. "Now go right," he goes right. I had him turning on a dime that night. We went to the pool hall, took in a movie. I tried to get him into a massage parlour, the one at the corner of First and King, but no dice—sex is one area where I can't get through. It kills me. Women are always coming on to us so they can say, I made it with the two-headed man. But Samuel doesn't believe in premarital sex. And his taste in women, it's enough to turn you into a fag.

A couple of years ago he got the hots for a dental hygienist. Six foot two, skinny, no chin, glasses. She's cleaning our teeth, acting like there's nothing unusual going on, and if there's one thing that burns my ass, it's people pretending there's nothing unusual going on. I mean, we've got two heads here! We've got show time!

Samuel's heart starts pumping. It makes me sweat. What does he see in her? I don't know. I don't care, either, because he's never asked anyone out. But fuck me if he doesn't invite her to a fellowship meeting!

I'm sweet as sugar. Give him the impression I like her. I've decided I want to see what happens. He buys a new suit, blue.

What happens is nothing. They go to the meeting, walk home, talk about the meeting, sit on the porch. She keeps trying to draw me into the conversation. It starts up that pressure above my left ear. Finally I tell her. "Show us your skinny tits or shut up."

"I beg your pardon?" she says.

"Samuel's getting hard," I say. "Samuel wants to fuck you in the ass."

She grabs her purse and runs off. Know something funny? From the back she reminds me of Jill St. John.

For most of my life I considered Simon inseparable from myself—my cross to bear, as I've said. And yet I had faith that one day the cross wouldn't weigh down so heavily. Foolishly I believed that Simon would come to accept his lot, as I had accepted mine.

He fed this belief. By remaining virtually silent and submissive for days, sometimes weeks, he would raise my hopes and nurture in me a feeling of profound pity. Our mother thought that he entered visionary dreams during these silences. In her mind he was a temperamental genius, and despite knowing that "temperamental" was much too benign a word to ascribe to his tantrums and crude outbursts, I made an effort, while she was alive, to see him through her eyes.

It was very difficult. I witnessed far more than she did. I saw that he lied to her face. I saw that the control he exercised in her company was entirely self-serving. Never would it have occurred to him that she was capable of loving him even at his most vile.

She was a true martyr, our mother, and in her gentle way she encouraged me to be one, too. When she cooked chili for him, I was meant to suffer in silence the inevitable heartburn. Until she died I never had to feed or groom him—she was devoted to these tasks—but it was understood that I would always serve his whims. I endeavoured to do so, taking my strength from her. There was no one more patient and humble.

Except, I regret to say, when she drank. Then, she was another person, Simon's confederate. The change in her personality was truly frightening. But I do not sit in judgement. I have read that alcoholism is a disease, and in any event her resistance was constantly under siege. He stormed at her to get out the bottle. He damaged my liver.

I have just added that to the list: "Drinking in excess, damaging my liver." Having spent most of my life ignoring Simon's incitements, I find it hard to call every one of them to mind. I am often distracted by pain. And by the silence. The silence is very strange, very foreign to me. I must confess that, blessed as his absence is, it will take some getting used to. Imagine my life. Imagine a head two inches away from your own, a head that, at its natural angle, faced into your right ear. Imagine feeling the heat of every breath the head took, smelling the odours of the mouth, suffering a permanent rash on your shoulder as a consequence of the mouth's drooling. Imagine the weight of the head, the strain to your neck and spine. Imagine not a moment's solitude.

And then, suddenly, solitude by the hour. In thirteen days I have seen my lawyer twice and the surgeon once, nobody else. I see nurses, of course, but they come and go quickly, they can scarcely be counted as visitors. For the most part, and for the first time in my life, I am alone. In this amazingly quiet room. The phone seems to be disconnected. Yesterday I held it to my deaf ear, purely for the sensation of being able to hold a phone up to that side of my head. When my shoulder has healed, I will see how it is to sleep on that side.

I wonder why the policeman outside my door never comes in. Perhaps he's afraid of appearing like one of the thrill-seekers he's been charged with keeping away. He has a smoker's cough. As do I, and there's something else for the list: "Chain smoking. Blackening my lungs and raising my blood pressure."

Occasionally the policeman whistles. I must have one of the nurses ask him to stop, for under the influence of painkillers I have imagined it to be Simon. Simon was a remarkably accomplished whistler, and as a rule I am partial to tuneful whistling, but when I hear the policeman I am overcome with an irrational terror that it is Simon growing back. He hated life, and you'd think he'd be glad to be gone from it, but he loved himself.

To my surprise I have been reflecting rather calmly

upon love these past few days. I have been approaching the subject from an intellectual angle, asking myself such questions as, What is love? What does the Bible mean by love? What kind of love is sanctified? I called our mother a true martyr because she loved Simon unreservedly, and yet I cannot help but think that loving anything so evil must be wrong. Love fosters and sustains its subject. Love is dangerously blind, pathetically vulnerable.

Simon knew all about that. For his own selfish purposes he courted love. In my case he was caught be-tween wanting me to love him so that I would be ignorant of his machinations, and wanting me to love him so that he might hurt me all the more deeply. By the time we were teenagers I was onto his games, and in any event he was tired of playing them. Before then, however, I occasionally succumbed to his charms. He had a knack in those days of divining my thoughts and expressing them with a beautiful simplicity that moved me to tears.

I remember one occasion, one night when I was nine, ten. I woke up from a dream that our mother had given me a leather jacket like Elvis Presley's. I was an ardent fan of Elvis's. Seems odd to me now.

The jacket in my dream was marvellous. It was decorated with two flowers on each shoulder. I woke up terribly depressed, because much as my mother doted on me, she would never be able to afford such a treasure.

I lay in bed for quite a while, expecting any minute to hear Simon complain that he wanted breakfast. But he said nothing until I was getting dressed, and then he said in a voice so wistful, a voice absolutely devoid of ridicule, "A leather jacket with four tulips was mine."

He can't even look me in the eye any more. He's shaving me, brushing my teeth, and our eyes meet in the mirror, he looks away.

Sure, it's guilt. The guilt of a Christian, nothing like it, nothing bigger and more off-base. Jesus Christ, I hate Christians. Always praying for something for themselves. When we were kids, Samuel would pray—out loud so I heard—that I wouldn't be there in the morning.

A real saint, Samuel. Carries around a Bible, suffers in silence. But let me tell you something. The saint around here is me. Hands down.

Because I'm guaranteed pure. I can't commit the three most heinous crimes, what the law and the Bible consider the three most heinous crimes—murder, theft, adultery. Shit, I can't even jerk off. No, that's crap, the thought is nowhere near as bad as the deed. Figure it out.

I'm not saying that Samuel has committed any crime, big or small. Not yet. Never even played with himself unless he did it when I was sleeping. What I'm saying is that even if he doesn't murder me (which he will), the potential to murder me or to commit any other crime is in him because he's got a body to commit those crimes with.

The body is a weapon. Samuel, and everyone else, is carrying a weapon, or how I think of it, they're carrying the seeds of crime.

Whereas I'm seedless. No potential, guaranteed pure.

The goddamn Virgin Mary.

Give me a cigarette. What do you know about Zen Buddhists? I heard how they think that if you contemplate something long enough, some stupid, simple thing, it doesn't matter what, but the stupider and simpler the better, if you just look at it and contemplate it, you eventually reach a state of holiness.

Say that's true. Then it's more proof that I'm the holiest son-of-a-bitch in the universe. Thirty-nine years I've been staring into his ear. I know every hair, every pore. Sure, I can twist my neck around, but straight ahead is facing his ear. I wake up, first thing I see is his ear. And there's nothing stupider than an ear. Nothing as callous, either. An eye, a mouth, a nose, they do things—wink, pucker up, sneeze. They communicate. But an ear only listens. Takes it all in, gives nothing back.

I dream I'm living in his ear. I'm small. The whole world is his ear. There's the tunnel into his head, but I steer clear of it.

My shoulder is suppurating, and what scabs there are, are swelling into lumps as big as plums. Healing nicely, the day nurse said.

Is she mad? I demanded to talk to the surgeon.

"We'll see," she said in that infuriatingly sunny voice with which nurses humiliate and punish.

Goddamn bitch. The words erupted like bile in my throat, but I did not speak them. I clung for strength to my pain. There is nothing else. Imagine a molten spike forever screwing into your flesh. No relief, not even in sleep.

As if I have not suffered enough. All my life I strove to carry my exceptional burden with grace and even with gratitude that I was so chosen. When at last I cast it out, my fury was the fury of Jesus casting devils through Beelzebub. Why is God punishing me for my act of ascension? Ascend! the scriptures command us. Ascend to the realm of purity!

Were it not for the letters I receive from strangers all over the world, I don't know how I would go on. Without exception the writers are sympathetic. They cannot understand the charge of manslaughter. A law student wrote, "It isn't as if the law requires a precedent against which all future self-decapitations will be judged." Many people have pointed out that it is the possession of a soul, not a brain, that defines the human being.

I have received seven offers to sell my life story. One of these came from a man who interviewed me years ago. He was a script doctor for "The Incredible Two-Headed Transplant," a film that hurt me to the quick for its depiction of the host head as a fat, pathetic dimwit. At least it correctly portrayed the parasitic head as malevolent. I have not seen the other two-headed movies, but I have heard that the parasitic heads in all of them are likewise malevolent, and this has led me to wonder whether the filmmakers knew of my situation, or whether it is simply understood that any parasitic intelligence must be a devil.

It was certainly not our poor mother's understanding. She called Simon the opposite, in fact—the angel on my shoulder, my guardian angel. I am sure that these endearments disturbed Simon as much as they did me. Toward the end, when she was hospitalized and of no further use to him, he told her, and I quote, to "cut the fucking crap." Tormenting our mother. I'm writing that down on the list.

My hand shakes. God Almighty, the pain, even to move my arm! The injections are no longer effective. I realize now that the nurses are drug addicts, injecting my veins with a sugar solution so that they can inject themselves with my morphine. That's why they won't let me speak to the surgeon, they're afraid I will blow the whistle on them. Although telling the psychiatrist who was here yesterday has done precious little good. "Is that what you think?" he asked, implying that I suffer paranoid delusions. A court-appointed psychiatrist, intent on proving that I am insane.

"I sought to rid myself of a monstrosity," I told him. "Surely you must applaud that. Surely there is no saner act."

"But was Simon yours to get rid of?" he asked.

"Who else's, if not mine?"

"Had he no right to existence?"

"Does evil have a right to existence?"

The psychiatrist's eyes shone. He is young, excited by polemics. "Suppose I grant you that Simon was evil," he said. "Suppose I grant you that he was yours to kill. Do you believe that by killing evil you rid yourself of evil? Is not the act of killing a thing, however evil that thing is, and however much it is yours alone, in itself evil?"

"No," I said. I said it uncertainly, for although I have

no doubts that killing an evil thing is imperative and good, I have serious doubts that it is possible. I cannot help but connect the agony in my shoulder with the remnants of his nature. Indeed, as the wound swells and foams like a witch's brew, I find myself more and more persuaded that he is growing back. Not even God could destroy Lucifer, and physics informs us that nothing in the world is lost, no element or energy.

I've been thinking of saying to Samuel, You want to waste me, I'll make it easy for you—hire a whore, sit her on my face and have her fuck me to death.

I give him a couple of more days, a week tops. He's got the idea in his head, I've read it there. Now, it's a question of provocation. The ball's in my court.

There's something else going on, though. He wants me out of the way, but at the same time he's worried about not being this big stoic any more, this big fucking deal, the one and only two-headed man. He wastes me, and he turns into a regular one-headed Joe, and maybe she won't be so interested in him then. Maybe, underneath, she's just another freak groupie.

Sure, I've told you about her. Karen, his fiancée. Ugly as sin, dumb, pushing thirty and still a virgin. Always trying to get on my good side. Take a couple of days ago. She insists on buying me a book. "Okay," I say. "Go to Core"—you know, that bookstore that sells porn —"and pick up a copy of *Hard on the Saddle*."

"Oh!" she squeals, "a western!"

Samuel knows what I'm up to, but he can't get it across to her, that's how dumb she is. So she runs right out and buys the book and comes back and starts reading out loud about jism and hot stiff pricks before she twigs.

Then she turns beet red, but fuck me if she doesn't keep reading! And the whole time Samuel's trying to get her to stop. And trying to hide the fact that he's got the hard-on of his life.

We met her at Folios, that café that sells books. We never used to go out all that much, Samuel was afraid of what I'd say. But, still, we went out quite a bit, considering. He gets a righteous kick, having people witness his suffering. Since the old lady died, though, he's been gagging me. It turns out that a gagged parasitic head still earns you a lot of sympathy, especially if you tell people that you have to control the head for its own good because it's prone to fits.

That's the line he used on Karen. Hooked her right in. Five minutes later he had her wanting to dedicate her life to him.

Christ, he really thinks she'll be happy married to him. He thinks that as long as he keeps me gagged, the two of them will be a happy, normal couple. Why the hell doesn't he just fuck her once in a while and leave it at that? The poor dumb broad has no idea what she's walking into.

Sure, I've warned her. The minute the gag is off, I say, "Hit the road." She just smiles, thinks she can handle it. She hasn't got a bad-looking mouth. You know Jill St. John's mouth? Like that. Tongue-kiss me, I tell her. She pecks me on the cheek. I tell her to let me eat her pussy. She keeps on smiling. You've got to hand it to her.

I have fired my lawyer for incompetency and betrayal of trust. All along she intended for me to plead temporary insanity. "But we agreed," she protested, as if the deception was mine, and such was my ensuing rage that I confess I rained invectives upon her.

I will act as my own defence counsel. I will confront my oppressors alone. Which is as it should be.

Where my strength comes from I cannot imagine. My prayers go unanswered, and the letters I now receive are either from hustlers or lunatics. My pain is past bearing. The wound has swollen up into one huge hideous boil, which everyone in this hospital pretends not to see, let alone be troubled by. Yesterday morning, at long last, the surgeon paid a visit.

"This is coming along fine," he said. "You shouldn't be feeling all that much discomfort."

I was flabbergasted. "Idiot!" I cried. "Open your eyes!" And then I saw that he had the cold, evasive eyes of the drug-addicted nurses, and I understood that he was in cahoots with them.

"Prepare my papers," I said. "I am going to check myself out."

"I'm afraid you are under house arrest," he said. "You leave here, you go straight into a cell."

The price of purity is abandonment. When Simon was on my shoulder I had moments of longing to be like other men. But I am not like other men. Less than ever, now that I bear resemblance to other men, am I like other men. How can men judge me? How can there be a jury of my peers? I foresee flagrant injustice. In spite of which I have been working on my case—by force of will alone pulling myself out of the fires of agony to write notes and make telephone calls.

At first I was surprised to find my phone connected, but then I realized, of course! They want to eavesdrop! When I pick up the receiver, before I dial, I extend greetings to the interlopers. "Hello, voyeurs," I say cordially. "Good afternoon, Satan's cohorts."

I try every hour to reach Karen, but she has bought herself an answering machine. "I will do my best to get back to you," she promises in the voice of a soliciting whore. Obviously she has already filled the gap left by me.

To think I almost married her! It is clear to me now that what I took for saintly patience was depravity. I chose to believe that she suffered in silence Simon's lewd remarks, whereas the truth is she welcomed them. Encouraged them! That is why she objected to him being gagged. I want nothing more to do with her, but unfortunately I must speak with her in order to prepare my defence.

Regardless of her version of the events of that night, I do not plan to exonerate myself on the basis that I was provoked by any particular action of Simon's. Granted, I acted in rage, but the realization that I must get rid of him had been growing in me for months. My defence will simply be that he was, and always has been, a devil embedded in my flesh, that he was an incarnation of what the scriptures enjoin every man to expunge from his being. My defence will be that it was my right—as it is the right and obligation of every man—to expunge my own evil.

A defence, by the way, for which Karen might thank her lucky stars. If I was provoked by Simon, then surely Karen was his accessory. On the night in question she called my gagging of him cruel, she fled in tears. I was so distraught that I bought a bottle of whiskey and drank most of it, and as I drank, Simon managed to chew off his gag. He then proceeded to rave with unprecedented sadism, blaspheming everything I have ever held dear—our mother and Karen, certainly, but also every fond memory, every hope and dream. It was horrible, unearthly for its thoroughness and intimacy.

He must have known what I was about to do, yet he persisted. Even as I picked up the saw, even as I held it to his neck. God in heaven, even as the blood sprayed.

I crave whiskey for its sedative effect. I cannot believe that anyone has ever suffered more pain than this. Clearly this growth on my shoulder must be lanced. It is pulsing with poison. If no surgeon will attend to it, I will do the job myself.

We're at a restaurant. It's two years ago. I swear I see Miss St. John, just as she's leaving. I tell the waitress, "Put a shot in that coffee, I thought I saw Jill."

The waitress says, no way. "You're brother's reading the Bible," is her excuse.

I've got two options. I decide on the cool one. The pressure above my left ear turns into burning while I wrap myself in mystery and dignity.

A dream comes back to me, the one about being a tree. Sap for blood. Limbs, so to speak. Nightmares about axes . . . tremors up and down my trunk. Autumn, on the other hand, doesn't worry me. I've gone through enough seasons to know that the dead feeling is temporary.

LIZARDS

I

THE MUSIC—The Pointer Sisters singing "I'm So Excited"—is way too loud. Some of the women are covering their ears. Hot Rod doesn't care. He struts around mouthing the words. He has disastrous teeth, crooked and bucked, and there's a gap on the upper left side where at least two are missing. Every time he reaches the end of the runway he flicks his tongue in and out and flutters his black cape to offer a glimpse of his long, pale penis. Emma is beginning to wonder if this is all he's going to do when he raises his arms and starts pumping his hips. His penis flaps around like a noodle. Women scream.

Not Emma. And not Marion, who can't seem to see past his acne. "It's all over his bum!" she shouts in Marion's ear when Hot Rod turns to face the wall.

"Watch out," Emma says. Hot Rod has suddenly leapt off the stage and is dancing in their direction. But it's the woman sitting on Emma's other side that he targets. Two inches from the woman's face he resumes pumping.

"The ones on his neck look like shingles," Marion says to Emma. She leans across the table to get a better look. "I guess you get what you pay for," she says, refer-ring to no cover charge.

"That's debatable," Emma says. She is referring to what Hot Rod has just said to the woman. She tells Marion: "He said, 'For ten bucks, I'll stick it in your drink.'"

Marion slaps a hand over her wine glass.

That was also the other woman's reaction. The woman is about Emma's age, thirty. She keeps shaking her head until, as if out of revenge, or conceit, Hot Rod wraps it in his cape. The woman's shriek is muffled. Hot Rod opens his arms, triumphant, then commences a frenzied, complicated flourishing of his cape as he backs up the three stairs and onto the stage. Under the fixed spotlight he turns away from the audience, lifts his arms and begins pumping his hips again. Faster, faster.

The music stops. Not the way it's supposed to but as if the needle jumped off the record. Hot Rod freezes, legs bent, groin thrust forward. A good thirty seconds go by and then the spotlight dims. Hot Rod still doesn't move. Women begin giggling and exchanging looks of uncer-tain hilarity, and Marion elbows Emma, but Emma is thinking that from the back and in this light, he's not bad . . . great shoulders, nice tight ass, long thighs . . .

The spotlight and the house lights come back on, and Hal, who owns the bar, yells, "Let's hear it! Hot Rod Reynolds, ladies!" Hot Rod leaps back around to reveal the semi-erection he managed while frozen, just a flash of it, then he hangs the cape over one arm like a toreador and strides off stage.

"Show him you love him, ladies!"

Generous applause, a few whistles. Even the woman who had her head wrapped applauds. (People in this town are so polite! When Emma and her husband, Gerry, moved out here from the city they had to learn that a stranger waving at you as you drove by wasn't waving you *down*.) What's going on now is more than good manners, though, as Emma realizes. It's that the women *want* to clap, they want to have-fun tonight, "Ladies Night," Hal has called it, substituting the Bear Pit's usual topless waitresses for what he says are Miami Beach boys. He says it now, trying to milk the applause. "All the way from Miami Beach, Florida!"

Marion crouches over her drink and says in her thrilled way that Craig, her new boyfriend, is going to kill her. She has a lovely, kind face and a grandmotherly manner that gives the pet store she manages a homey, animal-shelter atmosphere. What initially attracted Emma to her were her breathless accounts of horrific pet deaths. A border collie puppy goes missing when the hay is being cut and baled; months later, the farmer is breaking open one of the bales and out tumbles the dog's rotting, mangled head. A budgie is flying around the kitchen and lands on the hot wood stove, where, instantly, its feet melt like wax and its twig legs ignite and burn down to ash.

"I mean," Marion says now, "I thought there'd be, you know, whatchamacallit, jock straps." She extracts an embroidered handkerchief from her sleeve and blows her nose. "Why didn't you warn me?"

"I didn't know," Emma says. "The only other time I've seen guys doing this they wore G-strings."

That was seven years ago. On the same night Emma also saw female table dancers for the first and only time. She suspected that she was pregnant but hadn't had the test yet and hadn't told anyone, so she was still drinking, sharing a carafe of wine with Gerry on the patio of a downtown restaurant, right across the street from a new bar with a neon "25 Girls 25" sign. Gerry had heard about the bar from some guys in his office, and he said she wouldn't be able to take it, but she said she was going over whether he did or not.

It was like underwater in there, a murky pond. Dark, smoky. Quiet, since it was between stage acts. All around the room, like seaweed in the current, slender, naked women stood on little round tables and slowly writhed for men who sat right underneath them and looked up. The men hardly spoke or even moved except to reach for their drinks or their cigarettes.

As if nobody could see her (and nobody seemed to), Emma twisted in her chair and stared, while Gerry tried to get the attention of a waitress wearing a tight T-shirt that said "Better A Blow Job Than No Job." Emma asked him if he wanted to hire a dancer for their table.

"Is this some kind of test?" he said. He took a quick glance around. "You're the only woman in here who's not a dancer or a waitress," he said.

"I don't care."

He smiled at her and shook his head. She squeezed his leg. She was getting excited, not by the women's bodies (they aroused in her nothing but a resolve to lose weight), and not by what some of the women might be feeling. It was the men who were turning her on, what *they* were feeling. "Feasting their eyes," she thought, although they didn't seem to be getting any pleasure out of it. They were almost grim, in fact. It was as if they had finally got down to the true, blunt business of their lives. "Are there male table dancers?" she asked.

"Not that I know of," Gerry said. "Just strippers."

"I wonder if there are any of those clubs around here."

"Why?"

"Let's go to one."

He laughed.

"Why not?" She pushed the palm of her hand against his crotch. "Hey," she said, smiling. He was hard.

He smiled back but picked up her hand and returned it to her lap. "What'd you expect?" he said.

"Sweetie," she crooned, nuzzling his shoulder. He was still lean and ambitious then, in his stockbroker pinstripe suits. He still had an expectant look in his eyes. She is nostalgic for his eyes. She told her mother recently, and her mother said, "There was something lifeless about them, though. When he used to blink, I swear I could hear his lids click."

What Gerry would have said about his eyes was, "I was in paradise." Any mention of his old self and he'll claim to have been in a state of ecstasy then, before the accident. "The accident" is how he always refers to it, which strikes an odd note with Emma. *The* accident. She has noticed that he uses the definite article in a couple of other questionable places, for instance in reference to their marriage. "*The* marriage," he says. Also, "*the* weight," "when I lose *the* weight," as if she and obesity were two more bolts out of the blue.

When the waitress finally came over, Emma found out from her that there was a male strip club just two blocks away. The waitress took their orders but then disappeared for so long that Gerry said, "Let's get out of here," although a statuesque black dancer in horn-rimmed glasses was ascending the stairs to the stage.

Emma held back. "Oh, come on," she said. "This should be good."

"I can't watch with you right beside me," Gerry said, pushing his chair back.

"Why not? It doesn't bother me."

"But I wouldn't even come here by myself," Gerry said. He sounded unhappy.

So they left, but she steered him down the street to the male strip club. "You know, watching isn't fucking," she told him as they were going inside. "Dancing isn't fucking either."

"Right," he said. "And fantasizing isn't fucking. Foreplay certainly isn't fucking." He sounded as if he couldn't imagine what he was talking about.

The place was packed. Mostly women, but there were a few men. Emma and Gerry sat with four flashy black women at a table near the exit. The women were all using identical silvery cigarette holders, which they gripped in their teeth to free up their hands for clapping to the music—the theme song from "Quick Draw McGraw," Emma realized after a minute. On the stage, two men wearing cowboy hats, chaps, spurred boots and leather-fringed G-strings twirled lassoes and rode phantom bucking broncos and slapped their own asses.

"Gay," Gerry said in Emma's ear. He looked gratified.

Emma shrugged—maybe. That wasn't it, though. The fact that the dancers seemed gay wasn't why there was nothing erotic going on here. She folded her arms, disappointed. She tried to lose herself in the dancers' bodies, but their outfits distracted her. She could feel her whole self folding in, retreating from the light and noise, the idiotic music, the laughing.

The next act was a stripping admiral whose big finale was turning away from the audience, removing his G-string, then turning back around with his white glove waving on the end of his erection. Gerry laughed and applauded.

"Can we go now?" Emma said.

In the car they had an argument about whether the women in the club had been turned on. "They were sure acting like it," Gerry said. Emma said they were having a good time, but it was parody, it was women acting the way they thought men did.

"I'm a woman, I know how women feel," she said, and he granted her that, although she suddenly realized it wasn't true. She had no idea how other women felt. It occurred to her that she could be missing entire traits— irony and caution.

After leaving the Bear Pit, Emma and Marion go back to Marion's apartment above the pet store, and Marion admits that those are the only human penises she's ever

seen other than Craig's and her ex-husband's. She says
they makes her appreciate Craig's. "So what if it's not
all that big?" she says. "Who wants a Hot Rod or a Submarine—"

"There was no Submarine," Emma says.

"Well, what was the red-haired guy called?"

"Torpedo."

"Oh yeah, Torpedo." Marion pours coffee into china
cups with saucers. "I mean, who wants a torpedo in their
vagina, anyway?"

"Not me," Emma lies.

Later, driving home, Emma thinks of Gerry's perfect
penis and can't help wishing that he still had his perfect
body, more for his sake than for hers, though, because
the truth is she'd still be fooling around on him. Gerry
suspects, but he thinks it's Len Forsythe, and he thinks
it's over. He has no idea that it's still Len, and six months
ago it was Len's twin brother, Hen, and last week it was
a gorgeous nitwit who wore a hard hat (not in bed, but
everything else came off first) because he believed that
jet stream thinned your hair. Gerry wouldn't believe so
many guys if she showed him pictures, and what's the
point in him believing it? she asks herself. How would
that much truth make a man like Gerry happier, or better equipped to sell debentures?

In the three-person branch office where Gerry works,
he collects less than two hundred a week in commissions.
Emma means to cheer him up when she says, "It's not as if
you're knocking yourself out," but he blames the fact that
all his clients, inherited from a guy who retired, are dropping like flies. He usually finds out at breakfast, reading

the "Deaths" column in the *Colville Herald*. "Suddenly," he reads out loud, "in his eighty-fifth year ..."

Luckily, Emma's cat-grooming business has taken off, here where she figured she'd be doing all right if she broke even after the first year. Emma grew up in a place like this. She knows that pampering small-town cats means letting them sleep inside. What she didn't count on were all the lonely old women, some of them wives of Gerry's dead clients, who would gladly have spent a lot more money than she charges just to have somebody to talk to for forty-five minutes.

Because of her white coat and her stainless-steel grooming instruments, they take her for a medical person. They assume she will be interested in hearing the ghastly and humiliating details of their husband's last illness or of their own illnesses, and as it turns out she *is* interested, and her deep interest brings most of them back a week later with home-made cookies and bottles of jam and pickles and, incidentally, the cat.

Of course, there are also people who really do come for the sake of their animals. With them, Emma ends up doing most of the talking. They hover. To distract them from delicate procedures (cutting matted fur, cleaning out ears), she asks did they know that cats prefer Italian opera to country-and-western? That according to market research the more cats you own the more likely you are to wish that Sonny and Cher would get back together? She has acquired enough cat trivia to go on for the whole forty-five minutes, if it ever came down to that. Also cat stories—the Burmese that lived twenty-six months without water, the cat that was nursed by a spaniel and barked liked one, the two-headed cat, and then there all those cats that roamed thousands of miles to find their owners. If the client seems up to it, she tries out a couple of Marion's pet-death stories. "Did you hear about the tom that sprayed the high-voltage transformer?" is her best cat one . . . is the one Karl Jagger says made him want to unbutton her white coat and caress her breasts with the tail of his Balinese.

2

The initial attraction, Emma's father always maintained, were the tendons in her mother's neck, but he said that what swept him off his feet was the reptilian flesh between her fingers. When her mother was older he sighed over the splendour of her wiry, grey hair. He pushed together the skin on her thigh to see it pucker. "God, it's beautiful," he said, "like a peeled litchi nut." Her mother, who by then had learned not only to swallow the comeback but to fall right in with his strange raptures, regarded her leg as if it were a new and noteworthy landscape.

As a teenager Emma was in a continual state of mortification over these routines, especially if they took place in front of people. When her father started in on her mother or herself, that was bad enough, but he might go for anyone. He said to Emma's piano teacher, a cranky, vain woman devoted to her compact mirror, "Don't ever have that gold-crested wart removed."

"It's not a wart," Emma's piano teacher retorted. "It's a beauty mark."

"The gold-crested wart is the glory of the spadefoot toad," her father said.

Emma's friends assumed he was an artist of some sort—he had a goatee and longish hair, and all over the house there were naked figurines and gigantic abstract paintings and never fewer than six cats wearing brilliantly coloured collars from which dangled huge hand-made Algerian cat bells—but in fact he sold life insurance from an office in the basement. Over his desk was a photograph of Wallace Stevens, who had also been in the insurance business.

"My job," he told his clients, "is to convince you to part with money that you'll never see again as long as you live." On the chair where the client was supposed to sit there was usually a cat. Cats slept in the old-fashioned wooden file trays. If the client hated cats, Emma's father pretended to feel the same way. "Mind your own business!" he'd yell at a cat off in a corner washing itself. "Just keep us out of it!" he'd yell. "Okay?"

People either figured he was kidding (usually when he wasn't), or they were disarmed by the look of starry-eyed, unflappable love he planted on everybody. Or they bought wholesale whatever he said. They believed, for instance, that if every square inch of your skin was splotched with huge freckles you resembled the sun-dappled forest floor at dawn.

Emma considered herself immune to his doting rhapsodies. She might have thought she was a big deal when she was a kid, but she knew by the time she started high school that looking like a fruit bat wasn't something you bragged about. She was short and had a sharp nose and chin. Otherwise, she wasn't bad. She *did* have huge dark eyes and she remained proud of them. It wasn't until she left home and fell in love with a creep named Paul Butt that she discovered how much flattery she had actually bought.

For her size she had unusually long fingers and toes—like a tarsier, her father raved, and since "tarsier" sounded so exotic she went through her adolescence believing that everyone envied and adored her hands and feet. Then Paul Butt told her that Elvis Presley would never have dated a girl with scrawny hands like hers. He also said that her lips were too thin and that she should have electrolysis done on her arm hair.

She was so crazy about him that she underwent one agonizing electrolysis session, but even then, even at her most insecure, she never really saw herself through his eyes. Arm hair to him was still, secretly, "down" to her. When he dropped her for the electrolysis technician she blamed her father for making her unjustifiably vain.

Eleven years later all she can think to blame her father for is marrying someone so unlike himself, because she is convinced that a person's character is nothing more nor less than the battlefield where the personality of the mother and the personality of the father slug it out. When she told Karl Jagger this, at the beginning of their affair when they were indulging each other's confessions, he said that his parents were exactly alike, and he speculated that the complete absence of contention creates a personality vacuum in which the animal nature of the baby takes over.

"Wild?" she said.

"Black."

"Dark," she said, because he isn't black. Once, she asked him why he had never killed anybody, and he said, "Shackled by compassion."

Why she asked was that he makes a lot of money writing pulp fiction about ex-marines and decent police officers getting even with crack-dealing paedophiles and mutilators. In every one of the twenty-three books he's published, there are at least ten grisly murders, over two hundred and thirty in total, and he claims that no two murders are the same and that every one is described in authentic, meticulous detail. If some guy's brains are all over the sidewalk, he says, and it's winter in New York, those brains better be steaming.

It occurs to Emma that Karl and Marion might be made for each other, so when Marion and Craig break up just around the time that sex with Karl starts to get predictable, she tries to arrange a blind date. Karl is game, but Marion takes offence at being told she has something in common with a man who invents stories about humans slaughtering each other. She doesn't invent her pet-death stories, she says, and it's not as if she goes out of her way to collect them either. It's that being in the pet-store business and also the sister of a veterinarian she hears things other people wouldn't.

"I don't find them *entertaining*," she says.

"Well, no," Emma agrees.

Marion picks dog fur off her sweater, one of five pet-motif sweaters she knit to wear in the store. Emma regrets that Karl will probably never see Marion in this sweater with its psychotic-looking parrots all over it.

"I guess I'm just one of those people who are haunted by the gory details," Marion says.

"Yes, I know," Emma says soothingly. "I am, too." And she sees that there really is this difference between Karl and Marion, and between Karl and herself. Karl can laugh at what haunts him. She and Marion don't laugh.

There is something Emma can't stop thinking about.

Nicky was eleven months old. She was about to poke her finger in the new kitten's eye when Emma grabbed her hand and slapped it, something she'd never done before, and Nicky, after looking at Emma with more astonishment than Emma would have thought a baby was capable of summoning, slapped her own hand. Afterwards, almost every time she crawled near one of the cats, she would bring her finger close to its face, then pull her hand away and slap herself.

Sometimes this memory strikes Emma as a message from Nicky, Nicky telling her that the way to cope with the biggest shock of your life is to replay it until it becomes commonplace. Which is what Emma supposes she is doing, indirectly, whenever she reads supermarket tabloids or pumps Karl and Marion for the worst possible story, for the story that will reduce her own story to the status of contender.

3

She was still mourning Paul Butt, still sobbing in the washroom at the investment house where she worked as a typist, still toying with the idea of going to another clinic for more electrolysis, when Gerry came over to her desk wearing red track shorts and a shirt and tie, his suit pants draped over his arm.

"Emma," he said, reading the name plate on her desk. He'd only been at the firm a week, and this was the first time he'd spoken to her.

"Gerry," she said.

"Listen," he said, "I was wondering if you had a needle and thread. I've split a seam."

"Sure," she said sarcastically, opening her desk drawer, "I've got an ironing board, pots and pans, diapers . . ."

He looked as if she'd slapped him. "I'm only asking because I saw you mending something a few days ago," he said. "Your skirt—"

His eyes, she saw for the first time, were different colours—the left one blue, the right one gold. They were as round as coins and red-rimmed, almost as if he had on red eyeliner.

"Okay," she said. "Sorry." She caught him doing a fast skim of her body, and it came to her, like an illicit jackpot, that it wouldn't take much to win his life-long adoration. She found her matchbook needle-and-thread kit and held out her hand for the pants. "I'll do it," she said.

"No, that's okay," he said, shaking the hair out of his eyes. His hair was white-blond and very fine. Whenever he was on the phone he ran his fingers through it. Emma had watched him doing this. Her desk was to the left and slightly behind his, in the big room where all the brokers and typists sat, and she had watched him, not as prospective boyfriend material (she thought she was too heartbroken for that) but because he moved so enthusiastically, banging out phone numbers, racing his buys and sells to the order desk, and because he combed his fingers through his hair as though there was nothing like the feel of it.

"I'll probably do a better job than you," she said, coming to her feet. Then, before he could say anything else, she pulled the pants off his arm and headed for one of the empty boardrooms. "Won't take a minute," she called over her shoulder.

In the boardroom she lay the pants on the table. They were navy with red pinstripes. She was impressed by the creases in the legs. You could cut a tomato with that, she thought, running a finger along one of them. Her finger was not steady. What was the matter with her? she wondered. Why had she brought the pants in here? She could have sewn them at her desk. She held up her hand and tried to see if she could keep it from trembling. She couldn't. She investigated her forearm, the bald patch from the electrolysis treatment. Was that stubble? "Jesus Christ," she muttered, and she was afraid she was going to start crying about Paul Butt, but she didn't.

She picked the pants up. There was the hole, a big one, alongside and under the zipper. She stuck her hand through. She brought the pants to her nose and sniffed the crotch. Urine, very faint. Urine and the smell of steamed wool. With her eyes closed she took a deep, re-suscitative breath.

When she opened her eyes, Gerry was standing in the doorway.

"Oh, God," she said.

"I wanted to ask—" He stopped and shook his head and smiled at the floor.

She dropped the pants on the table. She gave a little laugh. In the other room brokers were picking up their phones on the first ring. She imagined sniffing the pants again and saying, "I smell trouble." She imagined sticking her entire arm through the hole and saying, "Wow!" She imagined throwing a chair out the window and it landing on a bus in which Paul Butt and the electrolysis technician were riding.

"I wanted—" Gerry began again.

"To ask me out," she said. She had nothing to lose.

After Paul Butt, who had figured that two fingers shoved up her vagina ought to do it and who said that only closet dikes wanted to be on top, sex with Gerry was instantly addictive. During the first six months they made love at least once a night, and then they moved in together and got married and made love most mornings, too. Then things dwindled off a bit when he started leaving the apartment earlier and returning later because of the bull market. It became a joke between them that *he* was the one who complained about having a headache or being too tired.

She was now working at home, grooming cats out of their second bedroom. She'd quit her job at the brokerage firm because management frowned on married couples in the same department. Her mother had wanted her to go back to university, but her father had said she should take up something serene and uncompetitive.

"Such as hawking life insurance?" her mother had asked in her customary dead-pan.

"Such as brushing her hair!" her father had declared, and eventually that led to the idea of grooming cats, starting with his.

Cat groomer. Emma liked the novel ring of it. She bought a how-to book, a white coat and some combs and brushes and scissors. She stapled advertisements to telephone poles and in laundromats, vets' offices and pet stores. Her first client, after her father, was an incredibly tall black man with a three-year-old daughter and an old Persian named White Thing, and at first Emma thought this was some kind of joke because the mats all over White Thing's fur looked exactly like the swarm of little pigtails all over the daughter's head.

A year later the black man and the cat returned. By then White Thing was matted again, and the daughter was living in New Jersey with her mother. By then Emma had had a positive pregnancy test, and Gerry had said that it made him feel weird during sex, as if they were going at it in front of their own child.

While she cut out the mats, the man, whose name was Ed, lounged on her couch, telling her how he hated his job as a policeman and was thinking of doing something to get himself suspended with pay. "Folding myself into the car is the worst part," he said. "Those seats don't go back far enough."

"So how tall *are* you?" she asked.

"Six eight."

She glanced at him. His limbs overhung the couch in graceful array. His eyes were bloodshot and characterful. They made her nervous and yet at the same time she felt distant from him, she didn't feel a thing. It reminded her of being X-rayed, not in the sense of him seeing through her but in the sense that a powerful and potentially dangerous procedure was being conducted on her body, and she didn't feel a thing.

When she was about halfway through he came over to watch her work. He smelled like an extinguished fire. The top buttons of his shirt were undone "You're just fine, baby," he said in a soft, low voice that rumbled through Emma like drums, and he might have been talking to White Thing, and he might have been talking to her. Either way, it would have taken a strait-jacket for her not to put down her scissors and slide her hand into his shirt.

He gave her a big smile.

She undid the rest of his buttons, moved her hand down to his stomach, over his buckle and against his crotch. He covered her hand with his and pressed and let go again, as if to make sure she hadn't missed anything.

She unzipped his fly.

"Feast your eyes"—he didn't come out and say it, but when his penis slapped into her hand like a relay-race baton, he was thinking it so loud she heard.

He visited her two or three times a week, but after a month, whenever they had intercourse, she imagined that his penis was thudding against her womb and denting her baby's skull, and she decided to call it quits.

By then she was way past guilt. Love had so little to do with what went on between her and Ed that it was hard for her to think in terms of betrayal. Her regret was that she couldn't amaze Gerry with the fact that Ed's penis changed colour, from mahogany when he was flaccid to dark purple when he was hard. She couldn't tell Gerry that whereas his testicles were smooth, Ed's had the texture of brain coral.

She wondered what her father would have compared Ed to—a crane fly, a racer snake. Gerry, her father said, was a glaucous gull because of his white-blond hair and the red rings around his eyes. Her father was crazy about Gerry's different-coloured eyes. Emma was crazy about his flawless, white skin. In the mornings sometimes, when he was half asleep, she ran her hand over his body and rubbed herself against his leg until she came. She did this with Ed, too, except that Ed was black and moving.

After she and Ed had parted company she figured that that was it for other men, at least until the baby was a few years old, but in her fourth month, two more prospects turned up. The first was the previous tenant of their apartment, whose junk mail, featuring free brochures for Craftmatic beds, had been cramming their mailbox and who knocked on their door one day asking if they had found five one-hundred-dollar bills in the medicine cabinet. They hadn't but she said they had and had given them to the Salvation Army.

"Fair enough," he said, moving her to tell him the truth and to invite him in for coffee.

He was a motor-home salesman, just transferred back to town. About thirty years old, jock's body, receding hairline, small blue eyes glued to her legs, small hands, which she was too inexperienced to know didn't necessarily indicate a small penis, the only kind she was prepared, at this point in her pregnancy, to risk. As she was expecting a client in half an hour, nothing happened, but before he left he managed to throw in that pregnant women were a turn-on, and he gave her his card in case she wanted to have a drink sometime.

Two days later, after four nights in a row of Gerry working late and then coming home and falling asleep in front of the TV, she was on the verge of phoning him when a red-haired guy arrived at her door carrying a cat he'd run over in the apartment-building parking lot. Somebody had told him she was a vet.

"It's dead," she pointed out. Its mouth was clogged with blood, and its eyes were open and blank.

The guy, who appeared to be in his late teens—black leather pants, leather jacket, motorcycle helmet dangling from his arm—held the cat up and said, "Oh. Right. Fuck."

"Come on in," she said. He looked like he was going to be sick. She took the cat and put it in a plastic Shoppers Drug Mart bag, and he sat on the living-room couch with his head in his hands, saying he knew the cat, it's name was Fred, it belonged to that cross-eyed teacher in 104.

"I'm sure it wasn't your fault," Emma said, but she figured it probably was, and she was suddenly so enraged that she had to leave the room. She washed her hands in the kitchen sink, then put the bag beside the front door.

"It was alive when I picked it up," he said. "It was alive, you know? It was alive right up until it died."

She sat in the chair facing him. His hands were small enough. On his fingers were silver rings and blood. His red curly hair was combed back and wet. He must have just had a shower. He was lean, the black leather slicked the long muscles of his thighs. "I'll tell her if you want," she offered.

He looked up, surprised. She expected him to say, "No, that's okay," but he said, "Would you? Hey, that'd be great. Thanks a lot."

So she went down to apartment 104, just in case the woman was home early from school. The bag weighed down, extraordinarily heavy. If the woman cried, she knew that she would, too, but nobody answered the door. When she came back into the apartment, the guy was checking out his reflection in the TV screen. She left the cat in the hallway and sat down across from him again.

"You're married," he said. "Right?"

"Right."

"Okay, I won't come on to you," he said seriously.

"Don't let that stop you," she said.

He lived two floors below her, on unemployment insurance. He came up whenever she phoned. They'd been sleeping together about a month when he said he loved her.

"You love yourself," she said.

He didn't argue with that. "I mean I really *love* you," he said.

"What you love is me making love to you," she said.

"Yeah," he said, nodding. "That's right," he said, as if he could rest his case.

"I've been thinking of stopping this anyway," she said. "I'm too pregnant. I can't bend over to pick up all the little red hairs you shed."

4

Nicky is fifteen months old. Ed, the black giant, shows up one day without White Thing. He's in uniform. When Emma pushes his hand off her ass, he laughs and says, "I guess you've got a baby crawling all over you, you don't need a man."

"As I remember, it was me crawling all over you," Emma says.

He offers to take her and Nicky out for lunch, a restaurant that features a roving clown blowing bubbles and dispensing prizes for clean plates. Emma has no clients until four, so she says sure, why not? "Aren't you on duty?" she asks.

"My partner's tied up and I've got some time to kill," he says, and she suspects that what he came here to do, his partner is doing somewhere nearby. Maybe not, though. Maybe his partner is conducting a drug bust or something. Or maybe this is just Ed trying to get himself suspended with pay. She doesn't ask. Since Nicky came along, anything dicey or unsavoury she'd rather not hear about. She is glad that she will be able to tell Gerry the whole truth—a former client dropped by and invited her and Nicky out for a bite to eat.

"We're going in a police car," she tells Nicky.

"Please car," Nicky says demurely.

Emma changes into a clean white blouse and a long white peasant skirt. She and Nicky sit in the back because Nicky's car seat is in Gerry's car. Nicky stands on Emma's lap and slaps the window. She is wearing a white crocheted sun bonnet, and at stoplights people notice her and look worried. "Funny if Daddy saw us," Emma says.

Ed is talking to his police radio, but he laughs and says over his shoulder, "It would teach him not to jump to conclusions."

At the restaurant the people ahead of them make way for Ed to pass through. "Hey," he says, staying at the back of the line. "I don't take bribes." There are bubbles rising from behind a high rattan screen, and Ed lifts Nicky onto his shoulders so that she can see the clown on the other side. When it's their turn to be shown to their seats, Nicky doesn't want to get down. "It's okay," Ed says. He follows the hostess. He is so tall that Emma can't reach Nicky's bonnet, which is slowly slipping off her head.

"What?" Ed says, half turning at the feel of Emma's hand on his shoulder.

"It doesn't matter," Emma says.

Ed suddenly yells something and stumbles.

Nicky flies from his shoulders.

Emma is splashed in the face. Half-blinded she turns. Nicky is on the floor, next to the wall.

"Get away!" she screams, punching at Ed. He falls on his knees and lifts Nicky's head, which is drooped too far sideways. His black hands lift Nicky's head. Now Emma sees the gash at the side of Nicky's neck. Blood pours out. Bright red baby blood. Emma presses her hand over the gash, the blood streams through her fingers. "Stop this!" she screams. Nicky's eyes flutter.

"We have to stanch it," Ed says. His voice is low and sensible. Emma tears at her own skirt. Her baby's head is falling off, but it's a matter of stanching the blood. She gives Ed her skirt and he quickly rips it and binds Nicky's neck. Nicky's legs jerk. Ed says it was the ceiling fan. Emma glances up—a silver blade, still spinning.

When Nicky was born, Emma's father stood at the window of the hospital nursery and loudly compared his caesarean-section granddaughter to the brown, trammelled-looking birth-canal babies. Nicky was a plum among prunes, he said. Nicky was a Christmas doll among hernias.

"We are all hernias, more or less," Emma's mother said in her sardonic way, which had a mollifying effect on the annoyed-looking relatives of the other babies.

Once Emma and Nicky were back at home, he often dropped by in the afternoons, sometimes with Emma's mother, usually not. If Emma had a cat to groom, he minded Nicky. He made tea for Emma's clients and sold them life insurance. One day he answered the door and it was the red-haired guy.

"Is that maniac your husband?" the guy asked Emma.

"I thought you'd moved," she said quietly. Her father had gone back to playing with Nicky.

"I was in the neighbourhood," he said. "So," he said, "I guess you're not up for any action."

She smiled. "No."

"Some other time," he said.

She started shutting the door. "I don't think so," she said.

It wasn't guilt, it wasn't tiredness, it wasn't worry that her father was listening. It was no interest. Since Nicky's birth she'd had zero sex drive. Which was natural, so her baby book said. Natural and temporary. "It'll come back," she told Gerry.

"Sure it will," Gerry said enthusiastically, although he didn't seem very disappointed that it was gone. Like Emma, he was all wrapped up in Nicky. They lay her on a blanket on the floor and knelt over her and kissed and nibbled at her like two dogs feeding from the same bowl.

Nicky preferred the floor to her crib. If they put her on the floor and patted her bottom, she stopped crying. Emma's father had discovered this. He was constantly trying things out on her to test her reactions and to nurture her perceptions. He carried her around the apartment and touched her hand to the walls and curtains and windows. He opened jars for her to smell. He warbled songs in what he claimed was Ojibwa, holding her foot to his throat so that she might pick up the vibration. One of the songs was apparently about how the toes of a baby's feet are like pebbles. After Nicky died, Emma couldn't stop thinking of her toes like pebbles. She raved that she wanted Nicky's foot, she should have kept her foot and stuffed it, and then she would at least have her foot.

"I don't know why I didn't think of something along those lines," her father said. "A couple of months ago I read about a taxidermist in Yugoslavia who preserved his deceased son and claimed it was a great comfort."

He was stretched out beside her on her bed. Emma spent all day in bed, and her father and mother arrived at noon with lunch and Audubon field guides and photography magazines that had torn-out pages (where there were pictures of babies, Emma suspected) and editions of the *American Journal of Proctology*, which her father subscribed to for its dazzling full-colour photos of the colon, photos that if you didn't know what you were looking at you'd think were of outer space.

Her mother straightened the apartment and returned calls on the answering machine. Her father turned the pages. Emma didn't know how he knew that looking at pictures was the only comfort, but it was. After her parents left, she slept until Gerry came home from work. In front of the television he wolfed down most of a family-sized bucket of Kentucky Fried Chicken. She lay on the couch and ate some of the french fries.

One night, during a commercial, he said, "I was thinking today about when you walked off the end of the dock."

When she was ten or eleven years old, before she could swim, she walked off the end of a dock because she was attracted by the shimmering water. She sat at the bottom of the lake and waited to be saved. It was a story her father enjoyed telling.

She looked at Gerry. "Oh, yeah?"

"I was just thinking about it."

He told her he didn't blame her. He didn't blame Ed, although she did.

5

A woman in Argentina puts her fifteen-month-old son on the potty and leaves the room. A toilet falls through the floor of a passing airplane, crashes through the roof of the house and lands on the child, killing him. "Tot Terminated by Toilet," the headline says.

"Are you through with this?" Emma asks, holding up the paper.

Marion doesn't look. She is picking up live mice by their tails and tossing them from their cage into a box for a customer who owns a python. He'll be in soon, the python wrapped around his shoulders. "Is that the one with the Siamese twins on the cover?" she asks.

Emma closes the paper. "Yep."

"Well, I was thinking of writing to one fella in there," Marion says. "Sounds up my alley, except that he wants long legs."

Ever since she stopped seeing Craig, Marion has been buying the tabloids for the personal ads. She confessed to Emma that last month she got up the nerve to write to a guy who described himself as a college-educated homebody and an animal lover. He wrote her back, on Ohio State Prison stationery, saying that he'd received forty letters and he'd need two pictures of her in the nude, a front shot and a back shot, so that he could narrow the field.

"But go ahead," she says to Emma. "Take it if you want. There's an article about crib death. About how classical music prevents it." She glances at Emma. "Hogwash, though, I'm sure."

"I played classical music for Nicky," Emma says, tearing off the page with the toilet article. She folds the page and puts it in her purse. "My father made a tape."

"Well, there you go," Marion says compassionately. She believes that Nicky died of infant death syndrome. When Emma and Gerry moved out here, they agreed that that would be the story.

"Mozart, Haydn, Brahms," Emma says. "All soft stuff."

Marion closes the cage and carries the box to the counter, where Emma is sitting on one of the stools. It's a wooden box with thin gaps between the slats. A mouse must be hanging on the side. A pair of feet, four toes each foot, emerge from one of the gaps and grip the outside of the box. Emma runs her finger along the claws, which are milky and curled like miniature cat claws. "I wonder if they know," she says.

"Oh, lord," Marion says, grimacing. The two of them have had the conversation, several times, about the obscenity of the food chain. They agree on these things. They agree that dogs laugh but cats don't. Fish feel the hook. They agree that there's an argument to be made for lizards—the ones with break-away tails that grow back—as representing the highest order of life.

It's Hot Rod Reynolds, the male stripper, on the phone. "Jay Reynolds" is the name he gives, but when he says he got her number from Hal, the manager of the Bear Pit, it rings a bell and Emma says, "Not Hot Rod," and he says that's right.

"You're kidding." She laughs. She's remembering his acne and the woman shrieking to be wrapped in his cape.

"So you caught my act," he says,

"Are you calling from Miami?" she kids.

"So, what d'you think?"

"About what?"

"My act?"

She takes a breath. "Why are you calling?" she asks. She suddenly has the sick feeling that Hal, a man she hardly knows, knows she sleeps around and has recommended her for a good time. She zeroes in on the guy who wears the hard hat as the guy who talked.

But Hot Rod says, "I've got a dog here looks half dead." He says he's been staying at the motel behind the Bear Pit, checking out the trout fishing, and there's this stray mutt he's been feeding and letting sleep in his room. He phoned the vet, but nobody was there. Hal said that she was a sort of vet.

"What's the matter with it?" she asks.

"It's foaming at the mouth. Panting like crazy. Hal thinks it's heat stroke."

She agrees. She tells him to put the dog in the bathtub and to run cold water over it. Half an hour later he phones back to say that the dog seems a lot better and to ask if he owes her anything. "Forget it," she says. But the next day he turns up at her house with a fish that he has gutted and wrapped in newspaper.

"If you don't want it, your animals might," he says.

She is struck by his awful teeth. "Thanks," she says.

"Emma Trevor, cat groomer," he says, reading the calligraphic door sign that her father made for her. He looks off to one side as if for no other reason than to present her with his profile. His hair is slicked back. His nose is upturned. His skin is almost clear—from being out in the sun, she figures. He is wearing tight blue jeans and an orange tank top and holding a cigarette between his thumb and forefinger. His teeth and unreasonable vanity she finds touching. As she expects a client any minute, she doesn't invite him in. "Come back in an hour," she says.

These days she takes precautions. Condoms. A warning that if Gerry finds out he'll blow the guy's balls off. "With this," she says, showing the gun. The gun was Gerry's father's, it isn't loaded, and Gerry wants to get rid of it, but Emma keeps it beside the bed, to scare off intruders, Gerry believes, and he's half right. If Emma feels guilt over other men it's when she tells this lie about Gerry, who is so gentle he not only won't kill the ants in their kitchen, he dots the counter with honey to feed them.

But the warning works. She can see that the guys are scared, although never scared off. Hot Rod asks if he can hold it, and when she hands it to him he dances around the room, gripping it in both hands, arms straight, and getting hard so fast she suggests he use a gun in his act.

He frowns, considering. "Too obvious," he says.

He's a noisy lover. He groans and makes weird yelping noises and thumps the wall with his fist. Which is why they don't hear the car pull into the drive or the front door opening. Gerry is right in the bedroom before they realize he's home.

"Jesus Christ," Hot Rod says.

Gerry bows his head. "Sorry," he murmurs and leaves the room.

Hot Rod lunges for the gun, rolls out of bed, throws open the window and tosses the gun into the neighbour's yard.

She accompanies Hot Rod to the door because she wants to retrieve the gun. The TV is on. As they pass through the kitchen she looks into the living room and sees the back of Gerry's head and his hand reaching toward a bowl on the end table.

"Will he come after me?" Hot Rod asks when they are outside. His tank top is on inside-out. His hair is shooting off in all directions. He looks goofy and very young, and she knows that anything she says he will believe.

"Probably not," she says. "Not if you keep your mouth shut."

He bites his lip.

"If I were you, though, I'd get out of town." She says it to deliver her line, to sound like the sheriff. She doesn't care if he leaves or not. Out here in the driveway, with the asphalt scalding her feet and the gun glinting in Mrs.

Gaitskill's rose bush, the possibilities of what might happen next seem endless and out of her hands.

"I was thinking of leaving tomorrow anyway," Hot Rod says.

She climbs over the split-rail fence and plucks the gun from the bush. If Mrs. Gaitskill has seen her, she has no idea what she'll say. She puts the gun on top of the fridge, out of sight, and then goes into the living room and sits on the couch. Gerry scoops a handful of potato chips from the bowl.

"God speaks to us in silence," the man on the TV says. He strikes her as a man who would either love you or beat you to death. Gerry seems arrested by this man. The notion that she has shocked Gerry into sudden religious fanaticism is preferable to what she is certain he's thinking.

"I'm sorry you walked in on that," she says.

Gerry switches off the TV and slowly turns his head. She sees his blue eye and then his gold eye and the redness around them that would appear to be from crying but isn't. She imagines Hot Rod taking credit for the pain and incredulity that have been in Gerry's eyes for five years, and now she is glad that he is leaving town.

"I don't know what to say to you," Gerry says quietly. "Except—" He glances at the blank TV screen. "Except that I don't want to lose you."

"You won't," she murmurs.

"I know I'm a fat slob," he says.

"God, Gerry—"

"It's just that I'd prefer it if you did it somewhere else."

She looks down at her hands, and there is Hot Rod's semen, dried and flaky on her palm.

"I'm not blaming you," he says.

She can feel the pressure building behind her eyes.

"Listen," Gerry says. "Whatever it takes."

That's it. That's what she knew he was thinking. She begins to cry. "This is not consolation!" she wants to shout. She has it in her to show him the semen on her hand and shout, "This is recovery! Do you want the truth? This is who I am!"

But she loves him. That is also the truth.

She cries without a sound. Presently she stands up and says, "I'll start supper."

"Okay," Gerry says. He turns the TV back on.

She sways a little. It's a sweltering day, she is burning up. If a budgie lands on a hot stove, its feet melt. There are a million truths. She understands that she has no idea which ones matter.

She is light-headed because she is pregnant. But she doesn't know that yet.

WE SO SELDOM
LOOK ON LOVE

WHEN YOU DIE, and your earthly self begins turning into your disintegrated self, you radiate an intense current of energy. There is always energy given off when a thing turns into its opposite, when love, for instance, turns into hate. There are always sparks at those extreme points. But life turning into death is the most extreme of extreme points. So just after you die, the sparks are really stupendous. Really magical and explosive.

I've seen cadavers shining like stars. I'm the only person I've ever heard of who has. Almost everyone senses something, though, some vitality. That's why you get resistance to the idea of cremation or organ donation. "I want to be in one piece," people say. Even Matt, who claimed there was no soul and no afterlife, wrote a P.S. in his suicide note that he be buried intact.

As if it would have made any difference to his energy emission. No matter what you do—slice open the flesh, dissect everything, burn everything—you're in the path of a power way beyond your little interferences.

I grew up in a nice, normal, happy family outside a small town in New Jersey. My parents and my brother are still living there. My dad owned a flower store. Now my brother owns it. My brother is three years older than I am, a serious, remote man. But loyal. When I made the headlines he phoned to say that if I needed money for a lawyer, he would give it to me. I was really touched. Especially as he was standing up to Carol, his wife. She got on the extension and screamed, "You're sick! You should be put away!"

She'd been wanting to tell me that since we were thirteen years old.

I had an animal cemetery back then. Our house was beside a woods and we had three outdoor cats, great hunters who tended to leave their kills in one piece. Whenever I found a body, usually a mouse or a bird, I took it into my bedroom and hid it until midnight. I didn't know anything about the ritual significance of the midnight hour. My burials took place then because that's when I woke up. It no longer happens, but I was such a sensitive child that I think I must have been aroused by the energy given off as day clicked over into the dead of night and, simultaneously, as the dead of night clicked over into the next day.

In any case, I'd be wide awake. I'd get up and go to the bathroom to wrap the body in toilet paper. I felt compelled to be so careful, so respectful. I whispered a chant. At each step of the burial I chanted. "I shroud the body, shroud the body, shroud little sparrow with broken wing." Or "I lower the body, lower the body . . ." And so on.

Climbing out the bathroom window was accompanied by: "I enter the night, enter the night . . ." At my cemetery I set the body down on a special flat rock and took my pyjamas off. I was behaving out of pure inclination. I dug up four or five graves and unwrapped the animals from their shrouds. The rotting smell was crucial. So was the cool air. Normally I'd be so keyed up at this point that I'd burst into a dance.

I used to dance for dead men, too. Before I climbed on top of them, I'd dance all around the prep room. When I told Matt about this he said that I was shaking my personality out of my body so that the sensation of participating in the cadaver's energy eruption would be intensified. "You're trying to imitate the disintegration process," he said.

Maybe—on an unconscious level. But what I was aware of was the heat, the heat of my danced-out body, which I cooled by lying on top of the cadaver. As a child I'd gently wipe my skin with two of the animals I'd just unwrapped. When I was covered all over with their scent, I put them aside, unwrapped the new corpse and did the same with it. I called this the Anointment. I can't describe how it felt. The high, high rapture. The electricity that shot through me.

The rest, wrapping the bodies back up and burying them, was pretty much what you'd expect.

It astonishes me now to think how naive I was. I thought I had discovered something that certain other people, if they weren't afraid to give it a try, would find just as fantastic as I did. It was a dark and forbidden thing, yes, but so was sex. I really had no idea that I was jumping across a vast behavioural gulf. In fact, I couldn't see that I was doing anything wrong. I still can't, and I'm including what happened with Matt. Carol said I should have been put away, but I'm not bad-looking, so if offering my body to dead men is a crime, I'd like to know who the victim is.

Carol has always been jealous of me. She's fat and has a wandering eye. Her eye gives her a dreamy, distracted quality that I fell for (as I suppose my brother would eventually do) one day at a friend's thirteenth birthday party. It was the beginning of the summer holidays, and I was yearning for a kindred spirit, someone to share my secret life with. I saw Carol standing alone, looking everywhere at once, and I chose her.

I knew to take it easy, though. I knew not to push anything. We'd search for dead animals and birds, we'd chant and swaddle the bodies, dig graves, make popsicle-stick crosses. All by daylight. At midnight I'd go out and dig up the grave and conduct a proper burial.

There must have been some chipmunk sickness that summer. Carol and I found an incredible number of chipmunks, and a lot of them had no blood on them, no sign of cat. One day we found a chipmunk that evacuated a string of foetuses when I picked it up. The foetuses were still alive, but there was no saving them, so I took them into the house and flushed them down the toilet.

A mighty force was coming from the mother chipmunk. It was as if, along with her own energy, she was discharging all the energy of her dead brood. When

Carol and I began to dance for her, we both went a little crazy. We stripped down to our underwear, screamed, spun in circles, threw dirt up into the air. Carol has always denied it, but she took off her bra and began whipping trees with it. I'm sure the sight of her doing this is what inspired me to take off my undershirt and underpants and to perform the Anointment.

Carol stopped dancing. I looked at her, and the expression on her face stopped me dancing, too. I looked down at the chipmunk in my hand. It was bloody. There were streaks of blood all over my body. I was horrified. I thought I'd squeezed the chipmunk too hard.

But what had happened was, I'd begun my period. I figured this out a few minutes after Carol ran off. I wrapped the chipmunk in its shroud and buried it. Then I got dressed and lay down on the grass. A little while later my mother appeared over me.

"Carol's mother phoned," she said. "Carol is very upset. She says you made her perform some disgusting witchcraft dance. You made her take her clothes off, and you attacked her with a bloody chipmunk."

"That's a lie," I said. "I'm menstruating."

After my mother had fixed me up with a sanitary napkin, she told me she didn't think I should play with Carol any more. "There's a screw loose in there somewhere," she said.

I had no intention of playing with Carol any more, but I cried at what seemed like a cruel loss. I think I knew that it was all loneliness from that moment on. Even though I was only thirteen, I was cutting any lines that still drifted out toward normal eroticism. Bosom friends, crushes, pyjama-party intimacy, I was cutting all those lines off.

A month or so after becoming a woman I developed a craving to perform autopsies. I resisted doing it for almost a year, though. I was frightened. Violating the intactness of the animal seemed sacrilegious and dangerous. Also unimaginable—I couldn't imagine what would happen.

Nothing. Nothing would happen, as I found out. I've read that necrophiles are frightened of getting hurt by normal sexual relationships, and maybe there's some truth in that (although my heart's been broken plenty of times by cadavers, and not once by a live man), but I think that my attraction to cadavers isn't driven by fear, it's driven by excitement, and that one of the most exciting things about a cadaver is how dedicated it is to dying. Its will is all directed to a single intention, like a huge wave heading for shore, and you can ride along on the wave if you want to, because no matter what you do, because with you or without you, that wave is going to hit the beach.

I felt this impetus the first time I worked up enough nerve to cut open a mouse. Like anyone else, I balked a little at slicing into the flesh, and I was repelled for a few seconds when I saw the insides. But something drove me to go through these compunctions. It was as if I were acting solely on instinct and curiosity, and anything I did was all right, provided it didn't kill me.

After the first few times, I started sticking my tongue into the incision. I don't know why. I thought about it, I did it, and I kept on doing it. One day I removed the organs and cleaned them with water, then put them back in, and I kept on doing that, too. Again, I couldn't tell you why except to say that any provocative thought, if you act upon it, seems to set you on a trajectory.

By the time I was sixteen I wanted human corpses. Men. (That way I'm straight.) I got my chauffeur's licence, but I had to wait until I was finished high school before Mr. Wallis would hire me as a hearse driver at the funeral home.

Mr. Wallis knew me because he bought bereavement flowers at my father's store. Now *there* was a weird man. He would take a trocar, which is the big needle you use to draw out a cadaver's fluids, and he would push it up the penises of dead men to make them look semi-erect, and then he'd sodomize them. I caught him at it once, and he tried to tell me that he'd been urinating in the hopper. I pretended to believe him. I was upset though, because I knew that dead men were just dead flesh to him. One minute he'd be locked up with a young male corpse, having his way with him, and the next minute he'd be embalming him as if nothing had happened, and making sick jokes about him, pretending to find evidence of rampant homosexuality—colons stalagmited with dried semen, and so on.

None of this joking ever happened in front of me.

I heard about it from the crazy old man who did the mopping up. He was also a necrophile, I'm almost certain, but no longer active. He called dead women Madonnas. He rhapsodized about the beautiful Madonnas he'd had the privilege of seeing in the 1940s, about how much more womanly and feminine the Madonnas were twenty years before.

I just listened. I never let on what I was feeling, and I don't think anyone suspected. Necrophiles aren't supposed to be blond and pretty, let alone female. When I'd been working at the funeral home for about a year, a committee from the town council tried to get me to enter the Milk Marketer's Beauty Pageant. They knew about my job, and they knew I was studying embalming at night, but I had told people I was preparing myself for medical school, and I guess the council believed me.

For fifteen years, ever since Matt died, people have been asking me how a woman makes love to a corpse.

Matt was the only person who figured it out. He was a medical student, so he knew that if you apply pressure to the chest of certain fresh corpses, they purge blood out of their mouths.

Matt was smart. I wish I could have loved him with more than sisterly love. He was tall and thin. My type. We met at the doughnut shop across from the medical library, got to talking, and liked each other immediately, an unusual experience for both of us. After about an hour I knew that he loved me and that his love was unconditional. When I told him where I worked and what I was studying, he asked why.

"Because I'm a necrophile," I said.

He lifted his head and stared at me. He had eyes like high-resolution monitors. Almost too vivid. Normally I don't like looking people in the eye, but I found myself staring back. I could see that he believed me.

"I've never told anyone else," I said.

"With men or women?" he asked.

"Men. Young men."

"How?"

"Cunnilingus."

"Fresh corpses?"

"If I can get them."

"What do you do, climb on top of them?"

"Yes."

"You're turned on by blood."

"It's a lubricant," I said. "It's colourful. Stimulating. It's the ultimate bodily fluid."

"Yes," he said, nodding. "When you think about it. Sperm propagates life. But blood sustains it. Blood is primary."

He kept asking questions, and I answered them as truthfully as I could. Having confessed what I was, I felt myself driven to testing his intellectual rigour and the strength of his love at first sight. Throwing rocks at him without any expectation that he'd stay standing. He did, though. He caught the whole arsenal and asked for more. It began to excite me.

We went back to his place. He had a basement apartment in an old rundown building. There were books in orange-crate shelves, in piles on the floor, all over the bed. On the wall above his desk was a poster of Doris Day in the movie *Tea for Two*. Matt said she looked like me.

"Do you want to dance first?" he asked, heading for his record player. I'd told him about how I danced before climbing on corpses.

"No."

He swept the books off the bed. Then he undressed me. He had an erection until I told him I was a virgin. "Don't worry," he said, sliding his head down my stomach. "Lie still."

The next morning he phoned me at work. I was hungover and blue from the night before. After leaving his place I'd gone straight to the funeral home and made love to an autopsy case. Then I'd got drunk in a seedy country-and-western bar and debated going back to the funeral home and suctioning out my own blood until I lost consciousness.

It had finally hit me that I was incapable of falling in love with a man who wasn't dead. I kept thinking, "I'm not normal." I'd never faced this before. Obviously, making love to corpses isn't normal, but while I was still a virgin I must have been assuming that I could give it up any time I liked. Get married, have babies. I must have been banking on a future that I didn't even want let alone have access to.

Matt was phoning to get me to come around again after work.

"I don't know," I said.

"You had a good time. Didn't you?"

"Sure, I guess."

"I think you're fascinating," he said.

I sighed.

"Please," he said. "Please."

A few nights later I went to his apartment. From then on we started to meet every Tuesday and Thursday evening after my embalming class, and as soon as I left his place, if I knew there was a corpse at the mortuary— any male corpse, young or old—I went straight there and climbed in a basement window.

Entering the prep room, especially at night when there was nobody else around, was like diving into a lake. Sudden cold and silence, and the sensation of penetrating a new element where the rules of other elements don't apply. Being with Matt was like lying on the beach of the lake. Matt had warm, dry skin. His apartment was overheated and noisy. I lay on Matt's bed and soaked him up, but only to make the moment when I entered the prep room even more overpowering.

If the cadaver was freshly embalmed, I could usually smell him from the basement. The smell is like a hospital and old cheese. For me, it's the smell of danger and permission, it used to key me up like amphetamine, so that by the time I reached the prep room, tremors were running up and down my legs. I locked the door behind me and broke into a wild dance, tearing my clothes off, spinning around, pulling at my hair. I'm not sure what this was all about, whether or not I was trying to take part in the chaos of the corpse's disintegration, as Matt suggested. Maybe I was prostrating myself, I don't know.

Once the dancing was over I was always very calm,

almost entranced. I drew back the sheet. This was the most exquisite moment. I felt as if I were being blasted by white light. Almost blinded, I climbed onto the table and straddled the corpse. I ran my hands over his skin. My hands and the insides of my thighs burned as if I were touching dry ice. After a few minutes I lay down and pulled the sheet up over my head. I began to kiss his mouth. By now he might be drooling blood. A corpse's blood is thick, cool and sweet. My head roared.

I was no longer depressed. Far from it, I felt better, more confident, than I had ever felt in my life. I had discovered myself to be irredeemably abnormal. I could either slit my throat or surrender—wholeheartedly now— to my obsession. I surrendered. And what happened was that obsession began to storm through me, as if I were a tunnel. I became the medium of obsession as well as both ends of it. With Matt, when we made love, I was the receiving end, I was the cadaver. When I left him and went to the funeral home, I was the lover. Through me Matt's love poured into the cadavers at the funeral home, and through me the cadavers filled Matt with explosive energy.

He quickly got addicted to this energy. The minute I arrived at his apartment, he had to hear every detail about the last corpse I'd been with. For a month or so I had him pegged as a latent homosexual necrophile voyeur, but then I began to see that it wasn't the corpses themselves that excited him, it was my passion for them. It was the power that went into that passion and that came back, doubled, for his pleasure. He kept asking, "How did you feel? Why do you think you felt that way?"

And then, because the source of all this power disturbed him, he'd try to prove that my feelings were delusory.

"A corpse shows simultaneous extremes of character," I told him. "Wisdom and innocence, happiness and grief, and so on."

"Therefore all corpses are alike," he said. "Once you've had one you've had them all."

"No, no. They're all different. Each corpse contains his own extremes. Each corpse is only as wise and as innocent as the living person could have been."

He said, "You're drafting personalities onto corpses in order to have power over them."

"In that case," I said, "I'm pretty imaginative, since I've never met two corpses who were alike."

"You *could* be that imaginative," he argued. "Schizophrenics are capable of manufacturing dozens of complex personalities."

I didn't mind these attacks. There was no malice in them, and there was no way they could touch me, either. It was as if I were luxuriously pouring my heart out to a very clever, very concerned, very tormented analyst. I felt sorry for him. I understood his twisted desire to turn me into somebody else (somebody who might love him). I used to fall madly in love with cadavers and then cry because they were dead. The difference between Matt and me was that I had become philosophical. I was all right.

I thought that he was, too. He was in pain, yes, but he seemed confident that what he was going through was temporary and not unnatural. "I am excessively curious," he said. "My fascination is any curious man's fascination with the unusual." He said that by feeding his lust through mine, he would eventually saturate it, then turn it to disgust.

I told him to go ahead, give it a try. So he began to scour the newspapers for my cadavers' obituaries and to go to their funerals and memorial services. He made charts of my preferences and the frequency of my morgue encounters. He followed me to the morgue at night and waited outside so that he could get a replay while I was still in an erotic haze. He sniffed my skin. He pulled me over to streetlights and examined the blood on my face and hands.

I suppose I shouldn't have encouraged him. I can't really say why I did, except that in the beginning I saw his obsession as the outer edge of my own obsession, a place I didn't have to visit as long as he was there. And then later, and despite his increasingly erratic behaviour, I started to have doubts about an obsession that could come on so suddenly and that could come through me.

One night he announced that he might as well face it, he was going to have to make love to corpses, male corpses. The idea nauseated him, he said, but he said that secretly, deep down, unknown even to himself, making love to male corpses was clearly the target of his desire. I blew up. I told him that necrophilia wasn't something you forced yourself to do. You longed to do it, you needed to do it. You were born to do it.

He wasn't listening. He was glued to the dresser mirror. In the last weeks of his life he stared at himself in the mirror without the least self-consciousness. He focused on his face, even though what was going on from the neck down was the arresting part. He had begun to wear incredibly weird outfits. Velvet capes, pantaloons, high-heeled red boots. When we made love, he kept these outfits on. He stared into my eyes, riveted (it later occurred to me) by his own reflection.

Matt committed suicide, there was never any doubt about that. As for the necrophilia, it wasn't a crime, not fifteen years ago. So even though I was caught in the act, naked and straddling an unmistakably dead body, even though the newspapers found out about it and made it front-page news, there was nothing the police could charge me with.

In spite of which I made a full confession. It was crucial to me that the official report contain more than the detective's bleak observations. I wanted two things on record: one, that Matt was ravished by a reverential expert; two, that his cadaver blasted the energy of a star.

"Did this energy blast happen before or after he died?" the detective asked.

"After," I said, adding quickly that I couldn't have foreseen such a blast. The one tricky area was why I hadn't stopped the suicide. Why I hadn't talked, or cut, Matt down.

I lied. I said that as soon as I entered Matt's room, he kicked away the ladder. Nobody could prove otherwise. But I've often wondered how much time actually passed between when I opened the door and when his neck broke. In crises, a minute isn't a minute. There's the same chaos you get at the instant of death, with time and form breaking free, and everything magnifying and coming apart.

Matt must have been in a state of crisis for days, maybe weeks before he died. All that staring in mirrors, thinking, "Is this my face?" Watching as his face separated into its infinitesimal particles and reassembled into a strange new face. The night before he died, he had a mask on. A Dracula mask, but he wasn't joking. He wanted to wear the mask while I made love to him as if he were a cadaver. No way, I said. The whole point, I reminded him, was that *I* played the cadaver. He begged me, and I laughed because of the mask and with relief. If he wanted to turn the game around, then it was over between us, and I was suddenly aware of how much I liked that idea.

The next night he phoned me at my parents' and said, "I love you," then hung up.

I don't know how I knew, but I did. A gun, I thought. Men always use guns. And then I thought, no, poison, cyanide. He was a medical student and had access to drugs. When I arrived at his apartment, the door was open. Across from the door, taped to the wall, was a note: "DEAD PERSON IN BEDROOM."

But he wasn't dead. He was standing on a step-ladder. He was naked. An impressively knotted noose, attached to a pipe that ran across the ceiling, was looped around his neck.

He smiled tenderly. "I knew you'd come," he said.

"So why the note?" I demanded.

"Pull away the ladder," he crooned. "My beloved."

"Come on. This is stupid. Get down." I went up to

him and punched his leg.

"All you have to do," he said, "is pull away the ladder."

His eyes were even darker and more expressive than usual. His cheekbones appeared to be highlighted. (I discovered minutes later he had make-up on.) I glanced around the room for a chair or a table that I could bring over and stand on. I was going to take the noose off him myself.

"If you leave," he said, "if you take a step back, if you do anything other than pull away the ladder, I'll kick it away."

"I love you," I said. "Okay?"

"No, you don't," he said.

"I do!" To sound like I meant it I stared at his legs and imagined them lifeless. "I do!"

"No, you don't," he said softly. "But," he said, "you will."

I was gripping the ladder. I remember thinking that if I held tight to the ladder, he wouldn't be able to kick it away. I was gripping the ladder, and then it was by the wall, tipped over. I have no memory of transition between these two events. There was a loud crack, and gushing water. Matt dropped gracefully, like a girl fainting. Water poured on him from the broken pipe. There was a smell of excrement. I dragged him by the noose.

In the living room I pulled him onto the green shag carpet. I took my clothes off. I knelt over him. I kissed the blood at the corner of his mouth.

True obsession depends on the object's absolute unresponsiveness. When I used to fall for a particular cadaver, I would feel as if I were a hollow instrument, a bell or a flute. I'd empty out. I would clear out (it was involuntary) until I was an instrument for the cadaver to swell into and be amplified. As the object of Matt's obsession how could I be other than impassive, while he was alive?

He was playing with fire, playing with me. Not just because I couldn't love him, but because I was irradiated. The whole time that I was involved with Matt, I was making love to corpses, absorbing their energy, blazing it back out. Since that energy came from the act of life alchemizing into death, there's a possibility that it was alchemical itself. Even if it wasn't, I'm sure it gave Matt the impression that I had the power to change him in some huge and dangerous way.

I now believe that his addiction to my energy was really a craving for such a transformation. In fact, I think that all desire is desire for transformation, and that all transformation —all movement, all process—happens because life turns into death.

I am still a necrophile, occasionally, and recklessly. I have found no replacement for the torrid serenity of a cadaver.

FLESH OF
MY FLESH

THE BED that Marion is lying on has a huge red Leatherette headboard in the shape of a heart. Marion remembers the headboard from when she and John Bucci came here. She remembers that the wallpaper—in this room, anyway, in the honeymoon suite—was turtle-doves. It's Eiffel Towers now, supposedly to go along with the new name, Bit O' Paris, except nobody calls it that. Everybody still says the Meadowview Motel, and when Marion went to the bathroom she saw they still had the old towels with the entwined M's on them.

There's cable TV, though—that's new. And this red duvet looks right out of the package. Marion has wrapped herself in the duvet because she suspects she's in shock. From owning a pet store she knows that if an animal goes into shock, the first thing you do is cover it with a blanket or your coat. Then you raise its hindquarters to counteract internal bleeding.

"Not that I'm in danger of internal bleeding," Marion thinks. "Lord knows."

She lets out a short, incredulous laugh. The kitten on her stomach rides the movement. It is completely black, black lips, pads, black inside its ears. Every three hours Marion feeds it formula with an eye dropper, then she puts it in the bathtub and tries to make it pee. Sam was the one who said they should bring it along. "You can't expect anyone else to get up twice in the night," he said, and she thought, What a wonderful man. Now she thinks that this was just him leaping at the prospect of diversion.

Where is he? He's been gone almost two hours, but she didn't hear the car starting up. She imagines him standing on the wooden footbridge where they stood after supper and waved at their fluttering shadows way down on the river. She asks the kitten, "Do you think he's okay?" and runs a finger down its spine. It frantically licks where she touched. Even its tongue has black on it—two black spots and a black tip.

"In the movie of my life," she tells it, "you can cross my path."

Marion had just turned nineteen when her mother was murdered. About a week after the funeral a white-haired secretary bearing two rabbit pies showed up from the school where Marion's mother had taught grade three. "Nothing this terrible will happen to you again," the woman said with such conviction that Marion snapped out of her hysterics, and from then on, whenever she found herself presented with some death-defying risk, she was inclined to take it.

Why she had become hysterical was that as she was

putting the pies down, she saw a piece of skin stuck to the side of the refrigerator. She knew immediately what it was, although up until that moment her imagination had steered clear of the smithereens her mother was blown into. She'd been away when it happened, visiting her grandparents in Ayleford, and then, by the time she got home, the police and detectives had come and gone, and the kitchen had been scrubbed down by Mrs. Mc-Graw, who heard the shots across three fields and claimed she knew from the sound it was no regular shotgun.

The murderer was a man named Bert Kella. He was the janitor at Marion's mother's school. At about eleven o'clock on Saturday morning, when Marion's father was in Garvey pricing wheelbarrows, Bert Kella drove to the house in his nephew's '67 Mustang, kicked in the door, shot Marion's mother twice from behind as she stood peeling potatoes at the sink, then shot out a living-room window and drove back to the school to drink a bottle of whiskey and have a nap. When he woke up he stole a tape recorder from the office and drove to the Catholic cemetery on Highway 10. He pulled over and started confessing. Marion never heard the tape, but her father did and there were excerpts in the papers. It was mostly a deranged ramble about all the stuck-up, cold-hearted "bitches" Bert Kella had ever met. It seems that he wrote Marion's mother a love letter, which she never mentioned to anybody and which, on the morning of the murder, Bert Kella discovered ripped to shreds in one of the school's garbage pails.

"That did it," he said on the tape. "It was like a concussion really. I am a bit scared now." Then there was the explosion of him shooting himself in the mouth.

The week before, Marion had signed her name to a Southwestern University application that her mother had filled out and more or less written the essay for. Her father had said he'd sever a couple of acres to pay the tuition. Her brother, Peter, who had graduated from the same university two years earlier and was now a vet in Morton, had phoned to say he'd show her around the campus.

That was the plan, but after the shooting nobody ever mentioned it again. Marion didn't even get an acknowledgement from the university, and none of her teachers tried to talk her into returning to high school and finishing her final year. In other words, and for reasons that weren't clear to her, she was off the hook, although she had trouble admitting this to herself until she was packing up her mother's suits and blouses for the Salvation Army. "They wouldn't have fit me anyway," she wept as if, otherwise, she'd have reapplied to Southwestern. As if the only thing standing between her and a professional calling was the plain fact that all these career-women outfits were two sizes too small.

Not going to school meant she didn't have to get up at six-fifteen to catch the bus into town. Now she slept until a quarter to seven, when she heard her father in the bathroom coughing up phlegm. She went downstairs and let out the dogs. After breakfast she did the dishes, made two sandwiches for her father's lunch, then had her shower. By eight-fifteen she was out the door. At four-thirty she came home and cleaned up the house a bit. Sometimes she saddled her mother's horse, Daphne, and rode her down to the highway and back. At five-thirty she started supper. On Tuesday nights her father went to the Legion Hall, so at some point on Tuesday she ironed a good shirt for him. After supper, on the other weeknights, she sat in her mother's La-Z-Boy chair and she and her father watched TV. When there was a commercial her father stood up because sitting was bad for his back. "Your mother was born with a hole in her back," he came out with one night. "Size of a penny."

"I didn't know that," Marion said.

"Above her hip." He indicated the place on his own back. "Right where the second bullet went in, as it happens."

A few minutes later, after he had sat down, he said, "That was just a fluke."

He was a big, sleepy-looking man, smart with machines and animals and not much of a talker. (Of course, Marion's mother had never let him speak. She'd say, "You tell it, Bill," and then carry on telling the story herself.) Because of a mild palsy, his head shook, normally only a little, but at the funeral it shook so emphatically that the minister stopped the eulogy and said, "Correct me if I'm wrong, Bill."

"You're doing just fine, Herb," her father told him in a calm voice, and he'd been talking calmly ever since. As devoted as Marion was to making sure he didn't break down in grief, she expected him to at any moment. She saw him standing in the middle of the yard one morning, his head bowed, his hands up at his face, and she thought, "This is it." Then he dropped his left hand and she saw the cigarette he'd been lighting against the wind, and she released her breath and returned to making his sandwiches, which is what her mother would have been doing right about then. Mrs. McGraw had told her that the police drew chalk outlines of her mother's remains on the kitchen floor, and every once in a while Marion was struck by the strangely comforting sensation that those outlines were fitted along her own skin.

During the hours that her mother would have been at school, she killed time by driving her mother's red Toyota on the concession roads, up one road, down the next, pretending that it was a job, a dire responsibility. Day after day she did this. Sometimes she drove at five miles an hour. Sometimes (remembering what the white-haired secretary who brought the rabbit pies said) she hit ninety.

Twice a week she visited Cory Bates, who had also dropped out of school and who lived with her parents in Garvey, in an apartment above a pet store. After saying, "I don't get what Bert Kella saw in your mother," Cory never again made any direct reference to the murder, and the last thing she did was treat Marion as if she were an object of pity. The opposite was true. "At least you've got a car," she said enviously. She said, "At least your parents aren't at each other's throats all night."

All day, Cory's parents slept. Occasionally one of them got up and used the toilet or ate something standing in front of the refrigerator. Their light red hair and Mrs. Bates's tallness and shifty green eyes seemed to discredit Cory's claim that she was adopted, but as Cory pointed out, paediatric nurses have an edge when it comes to finding a good match. A couple of years ago

Mrs. Bates had switched to looking after old people, and now she worked two nights a week in a retirement home. Mr. Bates was on disability. When Marion was there he never said a word, but Mrs. Bates was a complainer.

"The dishes aren't done," she said.

"I'm going to do them later!" Cory yelled in her amazingly thunderous and infuriated voice. Marion admired Cory for not sleeping all day herself, since she was always saying how tired she was.

"I'm an insomniac," Cory said. "It started when I was pregnant."

Her baby, a boy, was born a year ago and given to a couple who, by sheer coincidence, was also called Bates. When he grew up Cory said she was going to visit him and tell him what an asshole his father was. Although she didn't know where he lived she wanted to send him the German shepherd puppy from the pet store downstairs.

"A boy needs a dog," she said.

The puppy was the runt of the litter, the only one left. At night, when Cory's father and mother were fighting, it barked and cried.

"Its cage is right below where my bed is," Cory said. "And I swear to God," she said, "the minute it starts whimpering, my breast milk starts dripping."

Before going out, they usually stopped in to see the puppy. "Don't you want to just eat it?" Cory said. Marion poked two fingers into the cage and scratched its head. "Don't you want to just squeeze it to death?" Cory said, getting her entire slim hand through the mesh and wiggling the puppy's hindquarters.

They drove to the new Garvey Mall. Twenty-five stores sandwiched between a Woolworth's and a supermarket. At the Snack Track they ordered Coke sodas and fries and carried them to the mall's eating area. Most of the tables were occupied by retired farmers who smoked cigarettes and nursed a single cup of coffee all afternoon. Some of the farmers Marion knew, and normally they'd have asked her how she was bearing up, but one look at Cory and they left it at a nod. Cory was theatrically tall and thin, and she wore thigh-high black leather boots and jeans so tight she had to unzip the fly to sit down. When there weren't any empty tables she said "Fuck" loud enough to turn heads. Marion imagined Mr. Grit, who borrowed her father's Rototiller every spring, going home and saying to Mrs. Grit, "Bill Judd's girl is headed for trouble."

Marion didn't care. If anything, it touched her to imagine these decent men quietly grieving for her future. It comforted her. It was one of the mall's homely comforts, along with the slow, murmuring parade of shoppers and the light-hearted music and the intermittent rumble of the men's voices. Usually this atmosphere sent her into the same sweet trance that having her hair cut did, and so the fact is she hardly registered Cory's savage commentary on most of the women who walked by. The only time she really paid attention was when Cory used her as her point of reference—"Oh, my God, I can't believe it . . . that girl's wearing the same ugly sweater you have"—and even then (because a raving beauty to anyone else was an eyesore to Cory), she was never aroused or offended enough to make anything of it.

They sat there for at least two hours. Sometimes they got up and wandered through Woolworth's and the women's clothing store, but Cory didn't like to since she had no money to buy anything. If a newspaper had been left near their table, Cory turned to the classifieds and, in her loud voice, read the ads from the Help Wanted section.

"Experience in bookkeeping would be an asset. Must have a cheerful personality. Yeah, right. So they can walk all over you and gang bang you at office parties."

One day she picked up the paper but immediately threw it down again. "I should have kept the baby," she said. "At least then I'd be collecting mother's allowance."

"What about working for John Bucci?" Marion said from her reverie. John Bucci stopped by their table whenever he walked by. He managed the Elite Shoe Store, plus he was a partner in a gas station somewhere out on Highway 10 and he had an interest in a gravel pit.

"Forget it," Cory said.

"He seems like a nice fella," Marion observed.

"Nice fella," Cory mimicked. "Mafia drug boss, you mean. No way a guy his age—what, twenty-five, twenty-six?—no way he's tied in with all these businesses unless they're fronts for selling drugs."

This woke Marion up. "Oh, for heaven's sakes," she laughed.

"Okay, he's full of shit," Cory said. "One or the other. Anyway, I don't trust short, pretty guys."

But half an hour later, when he came by their table,

she pulled him onto a stool and asked if his gravel pit needed someone to answer the phone.

"Maybe, maybe," he said, nodding, twisting the gold ring on his baby finger and glancing around. "Not till after Christmas, though."

"I'll have slit my wrists by then," Cory said.

"Hey," he said. "I black out at the sight of blood."

"So I won't do it here," Cory said.

"Why don't you work in the store?" he said. His eyes were on the open zipper of her jeans. "This Saturday. One day, try it out. I need somebody this Saturday. Commission plus salary."

"Forget it," Cory said. "I hate other people's feet."

"It's their socks I can't stomach," John said. He looked at Marion. "How about you?"

"I like socks," she said.

Cory snorted.

"I mean, do you want to work in the store Saturday?" he asked.

"Oh." Marion was mortified by her mistake. "No, no," she said. "Saturdays I can't. Saturdays—"

"Hey." John patted her arm. "No problem." For the first time she noticed how black and sad his eyes were. Sad from his own mother dying, she thought. He had talked about coming to Canada with his mother and sisters, about helping his mother swab the ship's deck to pay their passage, even though he was only five at the time.

"Bullshit," Cory had said.

"It's true, I swear to God," he'd said. "My mother had arms like this"—he flexed his muscled arm—"from scrubbing other people's floors. When she was my age, she looked fifty. But she was beautiful, like a rose."

"Everybody thinks their slag-heap mothers are so beautiful," Cory had said.

It's midnight. Their car is still there. On the other side of the parking lot, outside the opened back door of the motel's bar, two waiters whip at each other with dish towels. A dog snaps at the towels. The dog, Marion decides, is an Irish setter/Saint Bernard cross. She knows dogs. Dogs are one thing she knows.

She closes the curtains, goes over to the dresser and reaches for the eye dropper and the bottle of formula. In the light from the dresser lamp she sees two bruises on the underside of her wrist. She checks her other wrist, and it has one big bruise. When she and Sam were standing just here, and she was starting to unbuckle his belt, he seized her wrists and said, "I don't have a real penis."

She laughed.

"Listen to me!" he said, and there was such a feverish, lunatic look on his face that she went still and then, disoriented, she swayed, and he tightened his grip. She said he was hurting her. "Sorry," he said, but his fingers didn't loosen.

"I'm listening," she whispered.

He said, "Okay," and took a breath.

While her hands turned white he told her the whole story, going back to when he was eight and lived in Delaware. "He's memorized this," she thought at one point.

She couldn't catch it all. There was only the astonishing crux. "Wait," she said finally.

"What," he said.

"I want to see it."

"No, you don't."

"I want to see it," she repeated calmly.

"It's a dildo, okay? You've seen a dildo before."

"I want to see it."

He released her wrists, turned around and opened his fly. She heard two clicks and then his fly zipping back up. When he turned back round he was holding it down along his thigh, concealed by his forearm. She glanced at his crotch, but he was wearing baggy pants—there was no confirmation of anything there.

"Let me see," she said.

He opened his hand.

They both looked at it.

"It's rubber," she said.

"Silicone, I think. I'm not sure, actually."

"How do you keep it on?"

"It attaches to a strap." He folded his fingers around it and dropped his hand. "I hardly ever wear it."

"I'm going to be sick," she murmured. Instead her legs gave out and she fell to her knees while he tried and failed to catch her, first with his free hand and then with both hands, dropping the dildo on the dresser, but it rolled off and down the side.

"Oh, my God!" she said.

Since the dresser was bolted to a panel at the back and couldn't be moved, he had to unbend a hanger to coax the dildo within his reach, an absurdly long and frustrating exercise that she watched in silence from where she had landed on the floor.

Cory didn't work in John Bucci's store on the Saturday he asked her to, but the next Saturday she did, and then in August she started working there full-time. Which meant that Marion only saw her Wednesday afternoons, when she came to the mall to do grocery shopping. Usually John wasn't in the store. Usually nobody was.

"I can't figure it out," Cory said.

Marion could. Cory scared the customers, not on purpose, but she was so forbiddingly tall and glamorous, slouched in the door, and her blaring "May I help you?" had old women patting their hearts.

Driving home from the mall one day, it struck Marion that the reason John didn't fire Cory was that he was in love with her. She looked at her stubby hands on the steering wheel and understood his craving for length. She pictured his and Cory's light-red-haired, black-eyed, tall and short children. She *saw* these children, preordained, spectacular. But the following Wednesday, another salesgirl was lounging in the doorway, and when Marion asked her where Cory was, John came out of the back room and said she had quit. "She got a job stripping," he said.

"You're kidding!" Marion said.

He smiled. "Okay, dancing. You want a job?"

"Dancing where?"

"Ask her." He kept on smiling. It wasn't the smile of

a broken-hearted man. "You want to go for a drive?" he said.

"Pardon?"

"You and me. Get some fresh air."

Her eyes plunged to his shoes. In her mind one black pointed toe shot out and kicked a drug addict who didn't have the money.

"Ah, come on," he said. "It's a like a summer's day out there. Beautiful. Beautiful as you."

She laughed.

"Hey, you're blushing," he said. "I like that."

He had a red convertible with the top down. Out on the highway the sun whipped her hair, but his black, combed-back hair didn't move. Seated, he was no taller than her. Remembering what he had said about fainting if Cory slit her wrists, she wondered if all virgins bled. Her heart flapped in her stomach, but it could have been the murder. Out of the blue her heart sometimes rocked her whole body, and she put it down to aftershock. What haunted her these days was the second bullet entering a hole her mother was born with. Her mother should have been facing the other way, considering that Bert Kella pulled up the driveway in a car with a rusted-out muffler and then kicked in the door. "Why didn't she turn around?" the police investigator asked. Nobody had an answer. "That's the sixty-four-thousand-dollar question," the investigator said.

John Bucci drove to the provincial park, and they got out of the car to climb up the cliff. "Wait'll you see the view," he said, wrongly presuming that she never had. She followed him up the path, which had been railed with logs to provide a stairway. He loosened his tie. At the top of the stairs he opened his arms like an opera singer and made a slow, revelling circle that ended up aimed at her. With his tie off she saw the two gold chains around his neck. "Isn't it beautiful?" he said. "I can't believe I'm here and you're here and it's so warm and beautiful."

She could feel herself blushing again. She turned and looked across the valley, where the tin roof of a house signalled out of golds and greens. A dog barked, probably from that place.

"Your hair is like music," John said.

"For heaven's sake," she laughed. She had tightly curled hair the colour of barn board.

"Like pianos," he said, stroking her head. "Like arpeggios."

She walked away from him, over to a deep crevice in the rock. Her skin felt as if it was being pelted by rain. She went right up to the edge of the crevice and judged the distance across.

"I saw a porcupine down there once," John said, coming up behind her.

Marion stepped back twenty paces.

"Hey, they don't throw their quills, you know," John said. She kicked off her sandals.

"Good idea," he said, and started undoing his laces.

While he was still bent over, she ran past him.

Fifteen years ago she had watched her brother make the same jump. She did it the way he did, in a long stride, in splits through the air, landing on a lip of rock that jutted out below the crevice's other side.

"Jesus Christ!" John shouted.

She grabbed a sapling to keep from falling backwards. John ran around the crevice and reached down to help her up.

"Jesus Fucking Christ," he said. "Why'd you do that? I can't believe you just did that." She let him pull her onto the grass. "You could have killed yourself," he said, dropping to the ground beside her.

"No," she said. "I knew I could do it." In fact, she felt like doing it again.

"But why the hell did you? I thought you were suddenly committing suicide or something."

"I just wanted to."

"You just wanted to," he said, smiling, shaking his head. "In other words you're out of your mind."

She lay back on the grass. "I don't think I am," she said seriously.

He stroked her face. He kissed the scrapes on her hand. "You're out of your mind," he said. "I love you."

He took off all her clothes but removed only his suit pants. The intercourse was so fast and painless she wasn't sure it had happened until she saw a coin of blood on the grass when he was off retrieving her sandals and she was getting dressed. She placed a yellow poplar leaf over the spot. He came running back, slapping her sandals together. Driving to the mall, he said that she was so beautiful, like a peach. He said again that he loved her. She couldn't tell if she loved him, not until the next day when she went to the shoe store and saw him kneeling over an old woman's foot and she remembered how as a five-year-old immigrant he had swabbed a ship's deck.

After she feeds the kitten she puts it in the bathtub and dabs a warm, wet washcloth under its tail. It bats at its pee streaming toward the drain. It jumps to feel her tears on its head. She picks it up and it sits alertly in her hand. She puts it on the pillow and opens the drawer of the bedside table and takes out the Bible. Whatever she turns to will be a message.

"And a woman," she reads, "having an issue of blood twelve years, which had spent all her living upon physicians, neither could be healed of any."

"Good heavens," she says, and then covers her mouth with her hand because the door is opening.

It's Sam.

"I came back," he says sheepishly.

She looks him over for a clue that could have told her. His narrow hands. Musician's hands, she used to think. He walks to the chair and sits with his legs spread.

"Did you always have an Adam's apple?" she asks.

He touches his throat. "Not like this," he says.

"Is that the hormones?"

"Yeah." He keeps his eyes on her. He's been crying, she can tell from across the room. Twice before she's seen him cry—when his dog, Tibor, was hit by a car, and when the girl picked up her father's shaving mug in the movie *A Tree Grows in Brooklyn*. Those times, instead of thinking "Men don't cry," she thought she was witnessing a side of the artistic temperament.

She looks down at the Bible, at the word "Behold." She says, "Well, I don't hate you. I didn't mean that."

"You have every right to."

Her throat tightens. "Is Sam your real name?" she asks.

"It is now, legally, but it's not the name my parents gave me." He runs his fingers through his fine blond hair, which is thinning at the temples because of hormone injections. Four years ago he started the injections. Two years ago he had a double mastectomy. His flat chest is the second thing she asked about.

"So what did your parents call you?" she asks.

His mouth twitches. "Pauline."

"Pauline?"

"Yeah." He gives an embarrassed laugh.

"Why didn't you change it to Paul?" she asks, and the reasonableness and inconsequence of this question remind her of how she and her father used to dwell on why Bert Kella shot out a window in the living room instead of in the kitchen, and before Sam can answer her she cries, "I can't believe this! I'm doomed or something!"

"Honey," he says, coming to his feet.

"No!" She waves him back.

He puts his hands in his pockets and turns to look out the window.

"You don't even have hips," she says, her voice snagging. She falls back on the bed. The kitten pounces over and purrs into her ear. They have no name for it because as soon as it weighs two pounds it will be for sale. When she can speak she says, "You should have told me."

"I know, I know," he says. "I just love you so much. And I thought—" He taps his nails on the arm of the chair.

"Thought what?"

"I thought it would all be over by now."

"What do you mean?"

"The surgery."

The construction of a penis, the last in a series of operations.

"You mean you were never going to tell me?" she asks, twisting around to look at him.

"Of course I was." He taps his nails. "You'd see the scars," he adds.

"Who else knows?"

He looks surprised. "Nobody. Well, the doctors."

"Does Bernie know?"

He shakes his head.

"Are your parents really dead?"

"They're dead," he says softly.

"You could have lied about everything," she says.

He looks straight at her. "Presenting myself as a guy might seem like a lie to you. But to me I am a guy. In every way except one, and that's going to change."

"Oh, Lord."

"Look, I knew you'd be shocked," he says. "I expected there'd be a big blow-up. But we love each other, right? I mean, I love you, I know that. And . . ." He blinks and looks down. "I can still give you pleasure."

She buries her face in the pillow. The hand that knew exactly what to do was a woman's hand. "Let's wait until we're married," he said every time her hand drifted down his body, down to what she flattered herself was an erection.

She starts crying again. "I thought it was something

spiritual in you," she says. "A vow to be pure or something."

He taps one nail, a steady, agitating sound, like a
dripping tap.

"I feel so stupid," she says.

"I'll never hit you," he says quietly. "I'll never shout
at you. I'll always love you. I'll always listen to you. I'll
never leave you. I'll never fool around on you."

She has to laugh. "One thing for sure," she says,
"you'll never get Cory Bates pregnant."

She began to see John Bucci two or three afternoons a
week plus Tuesday nights, when her father was at the Legion Hall. Because John lived with his aunt they couldn't
make love at his house, so they did it in his car. John
wanted to marry her, or at least to see her more often, at
nights especially, but he didn't push her, not at first.

"I admire you for putting your father's feelings above
your own," he said.

Which made her feel dishonest. All she was doing,
really, was trying to keep everything on an even keel.
Over the summer she had stopped sticking so faithfully
to her mother's routine, but she was still the woman of
the house, and having a boyfriend felt like having an
affair. "Maybe you can come for a visit in a couple of
months," she told John, thinking that by then her
mother would have been gone a year.

His family she had met many times—his aunt, his two
sisters, his four nieces and three nephews, his brothers-

in-law—because on Tuesday evenings, after they'd made love, he took her to his place for something to eat, and there was always a gang in the kitchen. The sisters raved about her the way he did. They told her she had the skin of a baby, and they said they hoped her and John's children came out with her blue eyes and dimples. They just assumed that she and John would get married and build a house on their aunt's property, as they themselves had done. They urged her to make John hire somebody named Marcel to dig the foundation. They affectionately counselled her to hit John if he didn't get the ball rolling. "Hit him with a stick!" they cried. "Hit him you know where!" With them she talked about her mother, since they talked so readily about their own. She knew from John that their mother had died in a car accident, but they told her how she had flown through the windshield and how in the casket her face looked like Dracula's, it was so stitched up. They cried, and she cried. "You are our sister," they said, which more than anything John said, or did, had her dreaming of marriage.

The aunt that John lived with, Aunt Lucia, wasn't so friendly. She couldn't speak English, for one thing. She glared from the stove and pointed at the chair that Marion was to sit in. She furiously circled her fist in front of her mouth if Marion ate too slowly. As Marion was on her way out the door Aunt Lucia usually thrust a jar of something at her—relish, spaghetti sauce—as if challenging her to take it, as if she knew that Marion would lie to her father about where it had come from.

"From Cory's mother," was what Marion told him. Her father had never met Mr. or Mrs. Bates and he probably never would, given their waking hours, so it was a safe white lie. Marion had phoned them three or four times to find out about Cory, but there was never any answer. She had finally gone to the apartment and rung the bell and knocked on the door. Still no answer.

"They're there, all right," said Mrs. Hodgson, the old lady who managed the pet store downstairs. "Every once in a while you hear a thump." She said that Cory left one morning on the Greyhound bus for Toronto. "Gussied up like a prostitute," she said without malice. "You know the way she does."

"What happened to that puppy?" Marion asked. "The German shepherd?"

"Oh, it died," Mrs. Hodgson said. "When I wasn't looking somebody threw in a dog biscuit laced with, oh, whatchamacallit, oh—" She snapped her fingers. "Arsenic."

"But that's terrible," Marion said.

"Yes," Mrs. Hodgson said vaguely.

"Did they ever catch the person?" Marion asked.

Mrs. Hodgson shifted on her stool. "Shut your yak-king!" she shouted at the parrot in the cage behind her. She turned back. "Poison's an awful way to die," she said. "Contortions and foaming at the mouth. But falling from a great height, that's what I'd hate the most. Knowing in seconds you were going to splat. I heard of this man, he was like a mad scientist. He threw live animals from apartment balconies to see how they landed. Naturally, the cats tended to land on their feet, even if they died. But I'll tell you the interesting part. The higher the cats fell from, the better chance they had of living. Because a cat has to straighten itself out in the air, and that takes time."

A couple of weeks later Marion was driving by the pet store and saw a Help Wanted sign in the window. On a whim she went inside and asked about it. It was part-time, Monday, Wednesday and Friday mornings, and seeing as she never saw John before lunch anyway, she decided to take it. She was prepared to be alone in the store (Mrs. Hodgson's plan was to do bookkeeping and chores at home), but more often than not, Mrs. Hodgson was sitting on the stool when Marion arrived, and she didn't budge until Marion left. While Marion cleaned cages and fed the fish and birds and played with the puppies, Mrs. Hodgson handled the cash and told Marion—and any customer who happened to be listening—her ghoulish stories. Most of them she read about in *Coroner's Report*, a magazine that her dead photographer husband had taken pictures for and that she still subscribed to, but she also had plenty of her own stories, many of which concerned animals. Cats put in ovens, dryers and dishwashers. Hamsters sucked up vacuums. A dog tied to the back of a car and forced to run to death.

One day, after describing the murder-suicide of a husband and wife, she said, "You probably know about that teacher out at Marley Road School, the one that was carrying on with the janitor and he killed her?" Then, before Marion could speak, she said, "What slays me is his name was something-or-other Killer. Bart or Tom Killer. Anyways, her husband was starting to get suspicious, so she decided to call it quits. Which sent Mr. Killer off the deep end. He stabs her forty-seven times I think the number was. Then he drives out to the cemetery on Highway 10, sits himself down on his own mother's grave, and shoots himself between the eyes."

"Good heavens," Marion said.

"For a janitor he sure made an awful mess," Mrs. Hodgson said.

What struck Marion was Mrs. Hodgson having no idea that she was Ellen Judd's daughter. She'd thought that everybody in Garvey either made the connection right away or was told about it soon enough. So that was a surprise, Mrs. Hodgson having no idea. As for her mother and Bert Kella being lovers, people had hinted along those lines before, but no one even slightly acquainted with her mother, or with Bert Kella for that matter, believed it for a second.

Marion decided not to straighten Mrs. Hodgson out. Somebody else would, sooner or later, although that's not why she didn't say anything. And it wasn't because she was too upset or too disheartened, either. Actually—and this was new for her—she felt disdain. "Stabs her forty-seven times," Mrs. Hodgson said, getting that essential fact so completely and elaborately wrong, and Marion thought, "Nobody knows." It was a thrilling, lonely revelation.

Eventually they fall asleep, Marion in the bed, and Sam sitting in the chair. Near dawn, screeching tires wake them both up.

Sam runs a hand over his face. "There's no sense in staying here," he says.

Marion looks at him. His blue shirt holds its colour

in the gloom. He has wide shoulders. You could draw his silhouette and pass it around and everyone would swear it was a man. Last night she believed she had no choice except to divorce him. Now she's not sure she even has what it takes to send back all the gifts let alone to come up with an explanation for the marriage ending on the honeymoon. "I guess we should just go home," she says, swinging her legs onto the floor.

"Okay," he says carefully.

"Glenda will think we don't trust her with the dogs," she says. Glenda is the retarded girl who works for her part-time.

"She'll be right," Sam says, laughing.

"Nothing is settled," she says sharply.

He gets up and goes into the bathroom. He's in there a long time with the taps running. She feeds the kitten. When he comes out, she and the kitten go right in. She manages to coax the kitten into peeing, then she sits on the toilet and flushes to veil the sound. Sam calls out that he's going to the office to pay the bill, so she decides to have a quick shower. Seeing her breasts in the mirror makes her cry. Everything about her from the neck down seems a waste now, and perverse, as if *she's* the one with the wrong body.

By the time he returns she is dressed and is packing the few things they unpacked. He says he thinks he'll have a shower, too. She sits on a lawn chair outside their door and eats wedding cake until the thought of him washing his female genitals crosses her mind, and she has to spit out what's in her mouth. A few minutes later he steps in it, coming out with the suitcases. "All set?" he asks.

In the car, neither of them say a word. At one point he clears his throat, making what strikes her as a prissy sound, and for the first time since he told her she has the horrifying thought that people might be suspicious. She remembers Grace saying, "Does he ever have long eyelashes!" She looks over at him and he's blinking hard. It means he's nervous, but she used to think he had a tic.

Her eyes fill. The "him" that she used to love isn't there any more. It never was there, that's the staggering part. And yet she still loves him. She wonders if she's subconsciously bisexual. Or maybe it's true that she loves blindly. When she kept protesting that she loved John Bucci—years after the divorce—her friend Emma, who was always trying to fix her up with a date, told her about an experiment in which a newborn chimp was put into a cage with a felt-covered, formula-dispensing coat hanger, and the chimp became so attached to this lactating contraption that when its real mother was finally allowed into the cage, it wouldn't go near her.

On Valentine's Day, John Bucci gave her chocolates in a black velvet case as big as a pizza box. Also a gigantic card with a photograph of a grandfather clock and the message "Time Will Never Change Our Love." She dropped the chocolates off at the pet store for Mrs. Hodgson to offer to customers. The card she took home in a shopping bag and hid in her underwear drawer. The next night, during supper, her father asked if she was seeing the Italian fellow who sold shoes at the mall, and her first stunning thought was that he had gone through her drawers, but it turned out that Mr. Grit had spotted her in John's car.

"Oh, well, I have lunch with him sometimes," she said, which was true. "He's a friend of Cory's," she added, which was also true, or had been.

"He sold me those maroon loafers," her father said. "Must have been three years ago now. Crackerjack salesman, I'll hand him that."

She didn't know what to say.

"Doesn't he have something to do with that Esso station out on Highway 10?" her father asked. "I saw him on the phone once. In the office."

"I think he's a partner or something," Marion said.

Her father pushed his plate away and took a cigarette out of his shirt pocket. When his head was shaking as much as it was tonight, he didn't light his cigarettes in his mouth. He held the match under the end until the paper and tobacco caught on their own. "Used to be a Shell station," he said, putting the cigarette between his lips and taking a deep drag.

"Oh, that's right," she said.

"Jack Kreutziger owned it," he said.

She nodded.

"Before that," he said, "there were the Diehls. Then before that, now this is going back, it was a restaurant. I remember you could buy two thick slices of roast beef, a mountain of mashed potatoes and a side order of fresh peas for a dollar forty-nine."

"A dollar forty-nine," she marvelled.

"Yes, sir," he said.

She could have told him everything—this burst of conversation was him putting out the welcome mat, doing his best to be both mother and father to her. Instead she stood up and began clearing the table. It wasn't that she thought he'd be mad or even particularly worried about her, that had never been the issue. Her mother might have had something to say about an Italian Catholic who drove a red convertible and wore gold jewellery, but all Marion could imagine her father saying was, "You should bring him around for supper."

Still, she didn't tell him, and although she was touched by what he was trying to do, and she was afraid he'd go away thinking he couldn't get through to her, it was John she felt guilty about. Ever since Christmas, John had been badgering her to give him an exact date when she intended to introduce him to her father. "Not until the end of February," was what she said at first, February second being the day her mother died. Now that it was almost the middle of February, she was thinking she'd better wait until after her brother's wedding in April.

"If you're playing games with me . . . ," John said, shaking his head.

"You can come around the day after the wedding," she said. "April twenty-third."

"I mean, if you're trying to tell me something . . . ," he said.

Lately he was accusing her of having hidden motives. When she got her hair cut short he said she did it to get back at him for flirting with the French girl who worked in his store.

"I didn't know you flirted with her," she said.

"I don't!" he shouted.

He accused her of thinking that selling shoes was low class. Otherwise, he said, if she'd wanted to work in a store, she'd have come to *him* for a job.

"But it's better for our relationship if I'm not your employee," she said. "Besides, I really love animals."

"I hate you working there," he said. "That old bag's poisoning your mind."

She let that go because it was probably true. Despite John saying "I don't want to hear about it," she couldn't resist repeating Mrs. Hodgson's grisly stories, usually to his enthralled sisters when he was in another room, but he always seemed to walk in and catch the worst part. He said she did it on purpose, as another way of torturing him. She kissed his clenched fist. She blamed his paranoia on herself, on the secrecy she was forcing him to live in. And her guilt was compounded by a misgiving that there was no real reason not to introduce him to her father, that there had never been any reason. This suspicion, and the prospect of losing him, gave her some troubled moments, although not so many that she moved up the April twenty-third date.

What moved the date up was something else altogether. The last Tuesday in March she arrived home early to do the ironing, and her father was waiting for her with a snapshot of a fat woman who seemed to be laughing her head off.

"Her name's Grace Inkpen," he said. "She's coming here Friday to spend a few days."

It turned out he'd been writing to her for five months. He had an accordion file of her letters, all of which were written in mauve ink on pale yellow writing paper. "You'll get a kick out of the letterhead," he said, showing her the drawing of an inkwell and quill pen and, underneath, a Michigan address. "Howdy Bill!" Marion read before he turned the letter over and let her read the newspaper ad, which he had cut out and taped to the back. "Queen-sized, happy-go-lucky widow," it said. "Country gal at heart, 54, seeks marriage-minded gentleman. Age, looks, unimportant, although teddy-bear type a plus. Will relocate. No games!"

"Of course, I'll always love your mother," her father said.

Marion looked again at the photograph. Glasses, fuzzy blond hair. Yellow Bermuda shorts oozing chubby knees. So different from her trim little mother that she said, trying to get it straight, "But you're not going to marry her."

Her father stacked the letters and tapped the sides and ends to line up the edges. "That's what she's flying up here to see about," he said, but he looked desperate, as though the whole thing had gotten completely out of hand, and Marion let out a laugh, then closed her eyes, overcome by a sense of the pure loneliness that must have driven him to this.

"Hey, listen," he said. "This is your home. If you don't take to her—"

"No, it's okay, Dad," she said. And it was only to reassure him that she added, "Because I think I'm going to be getting married, too."

So John Bucci came for supper the next night, bringing two bottles of red wine, a case of brown shoe polish and a stack of gas coupons. He wore his sharkskin suit. He offered to have his gravel company grade their driveway, and her father took him up on it. After he had gone, her father said, "His heart's in the right place," meaning he was prepared to see past the suit and big talk. Then, after a minute, he said, "That's what counts," and Marion got the feeling he wasn't thinking about John now, he was thinking about—he was selling himself on—Grace Inkpen.

He drove into the city to pick her up from the airport. He wore the charcoal suit he bought off the rack for the funeral. While he was gone Marion changed the sheets on the little trundle bed in her brother's old room. Last night she had offered to let Grace sleep in her room, which had a double bed, but her father had said, slightly alarmed, "She's not that big."

Well, she was. As soon as Marion saw her getting out of the car, she raced upstairs and gathered her brush and comb, her nightgown, slippers, pillow and the photo of her mother that she kept on her bedside table, and she threw them on the chair in her brother's room. Then she grabbed the pillow from the trundle bed and the vase of lilacs from the dresser and put them in her room.

When she got back downstairs, her father and Grace were still coming up the walk, Grace stopping every two steps to gaze around and exclaim. She had on a billowing pink coat and was holding a little artificial Christmas tree in each hand. "Bad boy!" she cried, laughing, when Sophie, their pregnant collie, leapt at an electrical wire dangling from one of the Christmas trees. Her father, who was carrying the suitcases, tried to kick So-

phie in the rump but he missed. An unlit cigarette hung
between his lips, and his head was shaking badly. Marion opened the door, and Grace, looking overwhelmed
with joy, came straight for her. "Well, well, well," Grace
said, rushing and panting up the steps. Marion backed
up a bit. "You okay with those cases, Bill?" Grace cried,
but her ecstatic eyes stayed skewered to Marion.

She gave Marion a hug. She was still holding the
Christmas trees. "I know who you are," she said. She let
go of her and shouted over her shoulder, "Why didn't
you say you had a pinup girl in the house, Bill?" Then,
"You can light that now!" She turned back to Marion. "I
upchuck if somebody smokes in the car." She laughed.

"I know how you feel," Marion said.

Grace used the point of one tree to push her glasses
up her nose. "Now these," she said, setting both trees on
the counter, "are for you, Mary Anne."

"Marion," Marion said shyly.

"Out of season," Grace said, "but what the heck, I
made them myself. That's my business, making Christmas trees. Where's an outlet? Where's an outlet?" She
picked up one of the trees and hurried over to the stove.
"There," she said, pushing in the plug.

"Oh, that's beautiful," Marion said. The tiny lights
shot off a rainbow of colours on the shiny metallic strips
the tree was made of. "Dad, look," she said.

"Hey, that *is* nice," her father said. He came over beside Grace, and Grace put an arm around his waist.

"Now's the time to tell you, Bill," she said, beaming
up at him. "Now that you brought me up here for my
looks and personality."

Her father stood there stiffly, giving her a smile that didn't make it to his eyes.

"I'm a rich woman," she said. "Oh, yes, oh, yes," she said. "You got a stack of Bibles, I'll swear on them. These here trees are a gold mine. I got a head office and five branch locations. I'm made of money."

Marion is taking it second by second. Will she tell Sam not to come up to the apartment? A second later it's, Will she let him unpack? While she's wondering, he goes ahead. In the interval between one second and the next, he moves in.

One morning she wakes up and they've been married two weeks. She can't believe it. She lives in amazement, perpetually in the first shocking moment. She's in a kind of torpor, which she and Sam are pretending is the dawn of acceptance. Maybe it is. Before going to sleep on the couch he kisses her lips, and she lets that happen. "I love you," he says, and she breathes shallowly and thinks, "What if we just go on like this?"

They never talk about it. If he still wears the dildo, she doesn't ask. She avoids looking at his crotch. The rest of his body she catches herself looking at for slip-ups, as if the real Sam is somewhere else and this one's a fake. She looks at him coolly and sometimes with distaste and wonder, saying to herself, "That's a woman's shoulder. That's a woman's arm."

And yet she knows that whoever he is he's who she loves. She knows that if she didn't love him, she wouldn't

know who she was. He listens to her. He's the only person who ever has, although until he came along she
didn't know that. Right from the beginning, whenever
she was telling him what she thought or felt, she had the
very real sensation that the breath of life was entering
her, just as if she were a flattened blow-up doll taking
shape. After he left the store she always felt lighter and
rounder, and a bit cockeyed. She remembers punching
the cash-register keys and the tips of her fingers feeling
ripe enough to burst.

Now, all the time, she feels limp, despite the love
being there. To her it's a miracle, her love. It's like the
one thing, the one little tree, that survives the otherwise
total devastation of a tornado. She's going by the restaurant where he works, and she sees him in the window
playing the guitar for nobody but the other two waiters
(he's the entertainment when it's not busy), she sees the
narrow curve of his back, and she would still stand between him and a bullet.

The only person who seems to have any idea that
something's the matter is her friend Emma. Everyone
else makes newlywed jokes and asks how the wedding
went. Glenda keeps asking when she's going to have a
baby.

"Never," Marion says.

Glenda smiles as if she knows better.

Emma, on the other hand, says, "Whatever you do,
don't get pregnant." This is after saying, "You okay? You
sure? You look like hell." One day she goes so far as to
say, "A marriage licence isn't carved in stone," and Marion loses her temper.

"What are you talking about?" she says. "I'm coming down with a flu bug and here you are herding me off to divorce court."

The idea of telling anybody, even Emma, is appalling to her. Here in Colville she has no fame. That has been the miracle of living in Colville. When she left Garvey and came here to live, all anyone knew about her was that she had enough money to buy the old plumbing supply building and turn it into a pet store and an apartment. She could laugh and nobody thought, How can she laugh? Eventually she could talk about her divorce from John Bucci because other people got divorced. Until she told Sam about the murder, not a soul knew that she had the nerve to open a store in a retail recession and to ice-skate on the Grand River during a thaw and to recount Mrs. Hodgson's pet-death stories without batting an eye because she was someone who had survived the most terrible thing that was going to happen to her.

She thinks that telling Sam was what made this other terrible thing happen. That talking about the murder here in Colville, where it had been under wraps for ten years, was like releasing a deadly virus. If it didn't instantly turn him into a transsexual (and who knows? It's not as though she hasn't witnessed the frailty of natural laws) then it did make her fall in love with him, the first man since John she goes and falls in love with.

Before that she wouldn't have dreamed that he'd be the one for her. He was the new man in town. The mysterious stranger, the catch. And then she started seeing him arm in arm with Bernie, a topless waitress at the Bear Pit. She saw the two of them kissing once, in the bank line-up, but the first time he kissed her, and she asked, "What about Bernie?" he laughed and said, "God, no. I mean, she's great, it's just . . ."

Marion waited. She wanted to hear it—the thing she could possibly have over a sexpot like Bernie. But all she got was, "She's not you," said so reverently, though, that she kissed him and told him she loved him, too, a delayed response to his declaration of a minute before.

She was still bowled over by it. If he'd come out with anything else, she would have started crying. She'd just finished telling him about the murder. The name Bert Kella hadn't crossed her lips in a long time, and it lingered in the air like a toxic gas that burned her eyes.

"He shot himself a few hours later," she said. "What my brother always says is, 'He saved me the trouble.'"

"I love you," Sam said.

She looked at him. He was blinking as if from a tic. "Pardon?" she said. He put down his cans of dog food, came around the counter, took her face in his hands and kissed her like a man digging into a meal. Between kisses he kept saying he loved her, but in a voice so full of doom that she figured he must have said the same thing to Bernie.

That tone of doom and everything associated with it—the looks of defeat, humility, anguish, the hesitation, the guarded answers, the withdrawing, the physical modesty (he wouldn't even take off his undershirt!) —she got wrong all the way down the road. With Bernie out of the picture her immediate sense was that some emotional deprivation, most likely the death of his parents, had left him with the idea that he didn't deserve love. So her job, her joyous crusade, became to persuade him that he did deserve it. He would sigh for no reason and she would say, "I love you." "I love you," she would say when she picked up the phone and it was him. He had a frailty she had never witnessed before in a grown man, not so much because of the way he looked, although he was slim and big-eyed, and not because he seemed frightened of loving her, either. It was something else—his dreaminess, partly, which she felt had to do with a spiritual bent, a private purity. Just as a room's perils leap out at you when you bring a baby into it, everything that was common and hard about living in Garvey seemed more evident to her whenever Sam was around. The very first time he came into the store and they got to talking, she'd wondered how anyone so open-minded would ever cope with the bullheadedness and rectitude of people here. When she'd started seeing him with Bernie, she'd said to Emma, "A racy girl like that will break his heart."

Her innocence! That's what floors her now. "What if I don't mind whether you respect me or not?" she said once.

"I won't respect myself," he answered.

"Then let's elope."

"We said we'd wait until I visited my relatives."

"What if I tear all your clothes off?"

"Let's just wait." (Moving her hand from his knee, coming to his feet.) "Okay, honey? I'm not cut out for this kind of thing."

That's exactly how he put it—he wasn't cut out for this kind of thing. In six months he thought he would be. Then there would be the months it took to recover. What he told her was that he wanted to visit his parents' grave in Delaware, then look up some relatives he'd suddenly heard of, get to know them, invite them to the wedding, and after that he wanted to do some camping in Vermont on his own. He'd be gone three, four months, he said.

But he misunderstood how complicated the operation would be. By the time he had the facts, and was therefore going on about delaying the wedding a few more months (he said his relatives might be away in the spring and it would be better to visit them in the summer), she was so sure that this was just him throwing up barriers between himself and his happiness, she wouldn't listen. She covered his mouth with her hand.

Sometimes she feels as if her hand is still there. Oh, they still talk. They tell each other about their day, that kind of thing. But whereas she used to tell him things she'd never imagined telling anyone else (even before they said they loved each other she admitted having faked her orgasms with John), now they talk as if their conversation will be played back in church. Neither of them goes near words like "orgasm" or "sex." She can't even say "love." She can't tell him that the ferret has gone into heat. She says, instead, "I'm going to have to get hold of Arnie," and leaves it to him to remember that Arnie is the guy out on Highway 10 who has a breeding farm.

She keeps wondering how long it can go on. The marriage, yes, but mostly how much longer they can keep up this uneasy peace. Then a letter arrives with a Boston postmark. She watches him read it. "Well?" she says from a state of calm that she can feel quickly giving way . . . to total rage or total apathy, she has no idea.

"I guess this is it," he says.

"You're not going to go ahead with it, are you?" she says.

He looks up, surprised. "Well, yeah. Of course. I mean, I thought that's what you'd want."

It's rage. It shoots up inside her like a geyser. "What *I'd* want!" she cries. "Why would I want that?"

He just looks at her.

"What on earth do you think? That all this time I've been holding my breath for a penis?"

He starts to speak but she cuts him off. "It won't be real!"

"It'll be real. They'll use my own skin and—"

"Oh, for heaven's sakes, it makes me sick to think about it."

"It won't ejaculate sperm—"

"Shut your mouth!" She actually punches him.

"But it'll get erect," he continues in the same instructive tone. "There's a way to do that."

She collapses on the little stool where they put on their boots.

"What if I lost a leg and got an artificial one?" he says. "Or if I had a glass eye, or, I don't know, a toupee, or I had a nose job? What about women who have breast implants?"

She shakes her head.

"What about fat people who used to be thin? What about Grace? You know what she said at the wedding?" His voice goes softer, more urgent. "She said, 'I don't know who this fatso is.' She said, '*It isn't me.*'"

Marion swallows around what feels like an acorn in her throat. "You just can't come into the world a woman and decide to be a man. That's what this all about. You can't do that."

He goes on as if she hasn't spoken. "Grace has the same dilemma I have. She knows who she is." He thumps his fist where she hit him, over his heart. "But she's in the wrong container."

Marion lets out a morose laugh. Grace as a container. "I thought I fell in love with a man," she says. "I thought I was marrying a man."

"You did," he says. "You did."

She lifts her eyes to his face. Against all the visible evidence, she says, "You're not a man."

He starts blinking. He lowers his head. He carefully folds the letter and puts it back in the envelope. When he looks straight at her again, she thinks he's going to kill her. "Who are you to say that?" he says quietly. His pupils are the size of pinholes. "Who are you to tell me who I am?" He reaches, and she flinches, but he's only pulling his jacket off the coat rack.

Her father and Grace were married in May, in Detroit, but they came back to the farm to live. It was a huge wedding, paid for by Grace, who waved away Marion's father's protests, saying, "The bride pays! The bride pays! That's the tradition!" and who arranged it all so fast and with such scouring efficiency, blasting the caterers on the phone while zooming out seams on her wedding dress (which she was sewing herself, using Marion's mother's ancient Singer), that all Marion's father had to do was stay out of the way.

After her second visit in early April she had moved in. She'd had her own phone line installed in the guest room, and she began doing all her Christmas tree business from there, sitting at Peter's little rolltop desk. When she wasn't on the phone—or sewing, or typing—she was baking. She showed Marion how to bake roll cakes and soufflés. She also painted the master bedroom pale yellow. She didn't even consult Marion's father, she just bought the paint and went ahead. "Green isn't my colour," was her explanation, not that Marion's father demanded one. With the paint that was left, she put a coat on one wall in the guest room. "I've got ants in my pants," she said. "I can't keep still." After supper, in front of the TV, she knit sweaters for Marion's father, multi-coloured cable knits that straightened his posture, he wore them with such pride.

He'd come a long way since that first visit, when her bossiness, her spectacular size, and especially the news that she was made of money, seemed to hit him like a shovel. That entire weekend he wore his neck brace to keep his head from thrashing, and after she was gone he fell into a kitchen chair and said, "What the Sam Hill have I gotten myself into?"

"I liked her," Marion said. She did. She liked Grace's good-natured self-awareness. When Grace had caught Marion's father staring at the way she loaded food into her mouth, she'd said, "This isn't a hormone problem, Bill. This is pure unadulterated appetite."

"I liked her laugh," Marion said.

Her father nodded.

"She's going to teach me how to knit," Marion said.

"You don't say?" her father said. He frowned and scratched under his neck brace. "All that money's something to think about," he said uneasily.

"For heaven's sakes, Dad. What if she were thousands of dollars in debt? Most people would say you've hit the jackpot."

"Well, I don't know . . ."

Something brought him around, though, something Grace must have written in the daily letters she continued to send. Because she came back. She came back with two trunks of clothes, a typewriter and eight boxes of business files. And three boxes of wedding invitations, already printed up.

The entire family plus six of her father's friends flew down for the ceremony in a private plane. John went as Marion's fiancé. He kept asking how much Grace had spent—he was comparing what they planned to spend on their own wedding in June, even though he had agreed to a small ceremony in the living room of Marion's house, where Marion's parents had been married thirty years before.

"What does it matter what she spent?" Marion said. Finally John leaned across the aisle of the plane and asked Grace. Marion cringed, but Grace couldn't have cared less.

"This here shuttle bus," Grace asked, "or the whole shebang?"

The whole shebang came to just under thirty grand. It was an amount that haunted John and more or less ruined their own wedding. He made last-minute changes, hiring a drummer and electric guitar duo who played so loud people had to go upstairs to talk. He had a canopy erected behind the house, a complete waste since it was a cool, rainy afternoon and there weren't enough guests to spill outside anyway. Because he was paying for the liquor he brought in crates of it and yelled at everyone to drink, drink. By the end of the night there was a line-up to be sick in the toilet. There was a fistfight between the drummer and the accordion player her father had hired weeks earlier. Marion's last memory, before she passed out on the trundle bed, was Aunt Lucia's bare stomach . . . Aunt Lucia with her red silk dress pulled up over her black bra, pointing at a snarl of purple scars under her navel and whispering, "*Guarda! Guarda!*" and Marion thinking that the scars had something to do with the birth of babies, that there was a Bucci baby curse Aunt Lucia was warning her about.

Apparently she was carried by John and her brother to John's car, and then carried by John alone over the threshold of the Meadowview Motel's honeymoon suite. They spent three nights there, a mini-honeymoon that John promised to make up for with a trip to Italy when he could afford to take some time off. From the motel they moved straight into their new house, a two-year-old five-bedroom, three-bathroom, white-stuccoed back split on ten acres. It had pillars on either side of the front door, a four-car garage, a sunken ebony bathtub and acres of white carpeting in which the imprint of a foot remained all day.

John had never had any intention of living on his

Aunt Lucia's property. He bought the house back in April, assuming a mortgage so high that Marion left off one of the zeroes when she told her father about it. Her father was still thrown for a loop. He and Grace gave them the five major appliances. The black leather chesterfield, two red velvet easy chairs, black veneer bedstead and black veneer dining-room suite John bought with the money his business associates sent in Congratulations cards. He wanted everything to be modern and either black or red. In a linen store in Ayleford, Marion found a red bedspread and black-and-red-striped pillow cases. She kept her eye out for coasters, towels, vases, lamps, ashtrays in red or black. She capitulated completely to John's taste because she didn't have any. Pointing out the dress she liked in a store window or in a catalogue had been one sure way to make her mother laugh.

She planted red and white carnations along the front of the house. She put in a vegetable garden. And three mornings a week she still went into the pet store. John wanted her to quit, but he said he'd let it ride until she got pregnant. Now that she was his wife, he was more easygoing about things, he was back to being his hearty, adoring self. He brought her long-stemmed roses and bags of seedless grapes. He wasn't home much—he liked to close the shoe store himself on the nights it was open, and he was always having to go to the gravel pit or the gas station to take care of some problem—but when he was home he followed her around, kissing her, undressing her, telling her how beautiful she was. He ran her bubble baths in the ebony tub and washed her breasts and belly.

Some mornings she woke up to find him looking at her, the two of them almost nose to nose, and it gave her a start because his eyes were so huge and inky. Moved by what she took to be his gratitude and amazement that she was finally his, she wrapped him in her arms and promised to love him forever.

A couple of times a week, when he was working late, she drove over to the farm and watched television with her father and Grace and knit John a sweater. Friday evenings she went to Aunt Lucia's to see John's sisters. Aunt Lucia still glared at her, but now she also pulled her out of the kitchen and made her feel the hard lump on her left breast, seeming to want to know if Marion thought it was growing, and one night she did a couple of knee bends to let Marion hear all the places her joints cracked—knees, hips, ankles, feet. It sounded like someone breaking up kindling.

"You're brother's a vet," John explained. "That's doctor to her."

"*I'm* not a vet," Marion said.

John shrugged. "Brother's close enough."

"Maybe she should see a real doctor," Marion said.

"In a million years she'd never go. Listen," he said. "She's old. She's gonna die soon. Humour her."

Marion was glad to. She was glad to be a Bucci, to belong to this large, passionate family. She was glad to be able to get away from them as well though, to drive back to her own ten acres and her enormous white house and its silent, mostly empty rooms. Its newness and splendour. She wished her mother could have seen it, could have seen how both she and her father had landed in clover. Maybe it was all her mother's doing, though.

That thought crossed Marion's mind a lot. Her mother still running their lives but with the power, at last, to go to town.

Her mother's birthday was the fifteenth of October. On the morning of that day Marion and her father and Grace visited the grave, Grace laying down a garland of white roses with a red ribbon that said "Gone But Not Forgotten." They all cried. "She had such a sweet, tiny face," Grace blubbered, and Marion wondered where she had got that from—her mother had been rather moon-faced, as Marion herself was.

In the afternoon, as Marion sat in her kitchen looking through her old photo albums, it started to rain. She got up to close the window over the sink and noticed that the raindrops were small spheres aligned in a plaid pattern so exact it looked like chenille. It looked like the kind of orderly message her mother's spirit might send.

No sooner did Marion think this than the phone rang.

"Hello?" Marion whispered into the receiver.

"Are you there?" a voice bellowed. *"Hello?"*

It was Cory Bates.

She was back in Garvey, calling from a phone booth. She had no place to stay because her parents had moved to Manitoba without telling her. She had no money. She had a black eye.

"Good heavens," Marion said. "Well, you can stay here until you find a place. We've got plenty of room."

"So I heard," Cory said. "I can't believe you married him. I mean, John Bucci! God! Does he wear his gold chains to bed?"

Marion had to smile.

"So, would he have a fit if I stayed?" Cory asked.

"Oh, no," Marion said, leaping at the opportunity to praise him. "He's really generous. He loves having people around."

"Yeah, so he can brag. I mean, I can't believe you even went out with him. But you've got a mansion and probably a new car, right? Can you come and pick me up? My feet are soaked."

Marion gave her the only other bedroom that had a bed. It also had an en-suite four-piece bath. Cory took a half-hour-long shower, then called Marion to come look at her two skimpy dresses, two pairs of jeans and three tank tops hanging in the wall-length closet. "Pathetic, right?" she said. She dropped back on the bed. She was so tall that although her head was on the pillow, her feet touched the baseboard. She lifted her head for a second to comb her fingers through her wet hair. It was jet black now, and cut an inch long all over. "Hand me those, would you?" she said, pointing to the pack of cigarettes on the bathroom counter. Her wide sleeve hung gracefully from her wrist. She was wearing an orange silk bathrobe, draped open below the crotch and showing off white, slender legs that made Marion think of the obscenely long stamens of tropical flowers. She gave Cory the cigarettes, and Cory offered her one.

"No, thanks."

"Still a saint, eh?" Cory said. "Well"—she smirked—"not exactly," and she scanned around her, implying that Marion was a gold digger.

So Marion told her about Grace, about all the money she'd actually moved away from to move in here. "Believe it or not," she said, "I'm really crazy about John."

"Christ," Cory said, flicking ashes on the carpet. "You know, I leave this shit-hole town to make some money, get a better life. I work my ass off . . ." She stopped and chewed on her bottom lip.

Marion didn't know what to say. "At least you're safe from Rick," was all she could come up with.

"Rick the Prick."

"I feel sorry for the lizards, though," Marion said.

Cory snorted. "I feel sorry I didn't flatten their warty little bodies with a hammer and put them in his cereal box."

Driving back to the house, Cory had told Marion how she'd landed a job at Rick's nightclub near the airport. A high-class place, she'd said. No nudity, strictly pasties and G-strings. Using her talents as an ex-cheerleader, she'd worked out an act in which she bounced on a little trampoline, doing somersaults and splits in the air, then cartwheeled over to a rail and performed a balance-beam routine. Within two weeks she was the headliner and had moved into Rick's twenty-fifth-storey penthouse condo.

Rick had two aquariums in which he kept lizards that shot blood from their eyelids when they were scared. Cory hated them, although she got a kick out of poking at them with a pencil. Evidence of blood in the aquariums was the only thing she and Rick had fights over, for the first six months, that is. Then Rick admitted he had fantasies of cutting her face so that no other guy would want her. Cory thought he was kidding until one night at a party he went after her with a paring knife. She forgave him because he was drunk and he missed her by a mile. But two nights ago, after she gave the bartender an innocent little birthday kiss, Rick tried to burn her with his cigarette lighter. She got away and ran right out onto the street, wearing only her G-string and pasties, and took a cab back to the condo. The first thing she did was pick up the lizards with hotdog tongs and throw them out the window. Then she stole the money on Rick's dresser—a couple of hundred bucks—and spent two nights in a hotel before taking the bus to Garvey. She'd told everybody she was from the West Coast, so she thought it would be a miracle if Rick found her.

"You know," she said now, running a finger under her blackened eye, "this place is even nicer than the condo."

"We're just thrilled with it," Marion said.

"I like it here," Cory said. "I wouldn't mind staying here forever."

She did, she did stay forever. At first it was going to be for two weeks. Just to get her out of the house, John rehired her in the shoe store, the plan being she'd save her wages to rent an apartment, but she didn't last three days. Selling shoes was too much of a comedown after being a nightclub headliner, she said. John let that pass. He just wanted her out. He thought she was a slut and was ruining their love life. No more bubble baths, no more sex all over the house, which Marion missed, too, but neither of them had the heart to tell Cory to leave. She had nobody else. She had nothing. John gave her some money for clothes to apply for jobs in, but she spent it on a black leather motorcycle jacket and black leather pants, claiming she didn't know how to dress like a hick. Waitressing at one of the town's two bars seemed to be the obvious solution, except that they were country-and-western and she said country-and-western music made her puke. John thought he'd finally found the solution when the hydro worker who rented the apartment behind the Esso station moved out.

"It's yours," he told Cory. "Rent-free until you get a job."

"Oh, great," Cory said, tears welling in her eyes. "A hole in the middle of nowhere where I can get raped by every greaseball in the county. Thanks a lot." And she ran into her bedroom and slammed the door.

Her insomnia had disappeared. She went to bed at nine or ten in the evening and slept until noon. Usually she was still in bed when Marion returned home from the pet store. She had long showers and watched TV and drove Marion's car to the mall, where she pestered John for cigarette money. While Marion made supper, she smoked at the kitchen table and cut to shreds whoever she'd seen that day, either at the mall or on TV. It was like old times, except that once in a while she went after John or his sisters or Grace, and even though Marion understood that this was just Cory trying to get her goat, she was nevertheless hurt and couldn't help rising to the defence, which was like throwing tin cans at a sharpshooter.

With Grace and John's sisters, her ruthlessness could take Marion's breath away. With John, however, she showed some restraint. She allowed for the other side of the coin. Okay, she conceded, John was generous and handsome...a generous bullshitter, a handsome shrimp.

One day she said, "I'll bet he's got one of those tuna-can cocks."

"He does not!" Marion said. "It's perfectly normal."

"How would you know? Have you ever seen another cock?"

"I've seen them on animals."

Cory burst out laughing. "Oh, right, you work in a pet store. Well, shit, I'm not saying that in a line-up of well-hung gerbils he couldn't hold his own."

Marion was furious. "I'm talking about horses," she said wildly.

Silence. A forsythia branch tapped on the kitchen window.

"You're kidding," Cory said conversationally.

Not long after that the snow melted under the bushes, and the warm air blowing over the fields began to carry with it the smell of manure and mud. Cory started getting up earlier to sunbathe on the front lawn in her pink-sequined G-string and a tank top. "Owooo, Mama!" John howled at her on his way to or from the car. Suddenly he was always running off somewhere, never home long enough to worry about whether Cory was looking for a job. So Marion stopped worrying, too. In fact, with John away so much, she had to admit that she was grateful for Cory's company.

Cory joined her now on her shopping trips for red and black things. She was an enormous help. "John will hate that," she'd say confidently, and Marion would pause and realize that Cory was right. After shopping they'd drive to the Bluebird Café for lunch. "On John," as Cory would point out, ordering dessert and an Irish coffee. She was gaining weight, but Marion thought she could do with it. Her hair was growing back to its lovely peach colour. Her eyes had their old shiftiness. She seemed to be over Rick, and one afternoon Marion ventured to tell her as much.

"*Over* him!" Cory said. "I hated that asshole from day one. You know, just because you live with some guy doesn't mean you have to like him."

"It does as far as I'm concerned," Marion said.

"That's *you*," Cory said. She downed her glass of wine. She lit a cigarette and looked out the window. "Stupid people get everything they deserve," she said fiercely. Marion assumed she was referring to Rick. "I have no pity for stupid people," she said. "I can't afford to."

Two days later, during one of the rare suppers that John was eating with them, Cory interrupted a story he was telling about a man with a quadruple-E shoe size and bunions the size of eggs. "I'm sorry, John," she said, "but she's going to have to know sooner or later." And she looked at Marion and said, "I'm pregnant and John's the father."

"Jesus Christ," John said, dropping his knife onto the floor. A full confession.

Marion watched him pick the knife up. The back of his neck was the colour of beetroot. "Why do I feel as if I already know this?" she asked, genuinely curious. She looked at her lifeline. It was long but forked.

"Listen—" John said.

"I'm not having an abortion and I'm not giving it up for adoption," Cory said.

John planted his hands flat on the table. "Okay—" he said. He took a deep breath.

"No way I'm giving it up," Cory said. "Not this time."

"Excuse me," Marion said, pushing back her chair.

"Hey!" John said. "Where are you going?" He followed her into the front hall. "Come on. Jesus. Where are you going?"

"Let her go," Cory said.

Marion never laid eyes on him again. He phoned her at the farmhouse three times that night, but she wouldn't talk to him. The next morning, while she lay on her old bed and wept, only letting herself really wail whenever the electric saw started up (Grace was having the kitchen renovated), her father and Grace drove to see him at his gas station. They told her nothing she hadn't figured out. John was confused. He still loved her. He wanted to do the right thing by the baby.

"How's he know it's *his*, that's what I kept harping on," Grace said.

"It's his," Marion said. Hadn't she foreseen John and Cory's children?

And yet she waited for him to knock the door down, to beg her to come back. When he phoned he said he loved her, then started crying and couldn't speak. She hung up. One day she stayed on the line to ask, "Do you love Cory?"

"Not . . . not . . . not . . . ," he said.

She waited.

"Not as much as you."

She dropped the phone and went into the bathroom

and considered the bottle of codeine. It wasn't worse than when her mother died. Her body didn't have that thin, hollow sensation of being made of crêpe paper. And the pain wasn't non-stop. There were hours at a time when she felt fine, even relieved. Compared to her mother dying it could feel like nothing, but it could also remind her of her mother dying. Force her—especially when she was falling asleep or just waking up—to see the piece of skin on the refrigerator and the skirts and blouses flattened in boxes for the Salvation Army. It was like being an alcoholic, and somebody gives you a drink.

What helped was going into work six days a week. She sat with the beagle puppies in her lap and tried not to pray it was John every time the bell on the door announced a customer. When she finally let Mrs. Hodgson know what was wrong, Mrs. Hodgson said, "Here's one that'll cheer you up" and told her about a woman who stole her best friend's husband, moved into the marital house and a week later was fried to a crisp when the furnace exploded.

Thereafter Mrs. Hodgson's idea of lifting Marion's spirits was reporting on any sightings of Cory in town. Cory was seen at the liquor store "loading up." At the drugstore buying a tube of lipstick with a hundred-dollar bill. One day Marion herself saw her. Cory walked in front of the car when Marion was stopped at a red light. She was wearing blue-jean shorts and Marion's red-and-blue plaid shirt rolled up at the sleeves and knotted under the tender swell of her belly.

That evening Marion phoned John at the store, the

first time she'd phoned him. She was crying. She didn't know what she was going to say.

But Cory answered. "Is that you, Marion?" she shouted after saying hello three times.

Marion covered the mouthpiece with her hand.

"Listen, Marion," Cory shouted. "You know, it's not as if he wasn't fucking half the jail bait in town!"

Suddenly another voice cried, "That's a lie, and you know it!" It was Grace, on the extension. "You're a liar and a home wrecker, that's what you are!"

Marion hung up. A few minutes later Grace came pounding down the stairs. "I wasn't eavesdropping," she said. "I was just about to dial out." She was panting and her face was startlingly red. "Holy mackerel, is she ever a stinker."

"I want to go away," Marion said. "I want to live somewhere else."

"Oh," Grace said. They looked at each other. "Where?" she asked.

"I don't know. Far enough from here that nobody will know who I am."

Grace pushed her glasses up her nose. "Well, I can't say as I don't know the feeling," she said.

The night before Sam leaves to have his operation, Marion dreams about somebody who starts out being her mother but seems to change into John. Marion is embracing this person, melting with love, when she discovers a hole in the small of his or her back. She sticks her hand in, reaches up and withdraws the heart. It pulses and half-rolls in her palm like a newly hatched bird. It is so exposed! She puts it in her mouth and tries to get it down her throat into her ribcage without scraping its delicate membrane or stopping its beat. It catches on something though, a tooth-like thing in the area of her vocal cords, and tears in half. She lets go of it and it just slips away. She starts to cry. She wakes up crying.

She buries her face in the pillow so that Sam won't hear. She wants her mother. *She* knows better, but year after year her heart goes on pumping out love as if all it knows is circulation, as if the beloved is right there in front of her to receive the love and purify it and send it back. She tries to envision her mother's face, but she can't. Instead she sees the heart she extracted in her dream. Then she sees an erect penis, a solid, ordinary thing, like a bird perch. Then a face—Sam's face.

He's standing in the doorway. She can feel him there. She opens her eyes but it's so dark it doesn't make any difference. He sits on the bed and begins to stroke her hair and her back. His hand draws the grief into his own hand, draws it in, lets it go. When she finally calms down, he slips under the sheet and lies beside her. Her bare back just touches his bare chest. She doesn't move away. She is so grateful for the solid, living length of him.

Neither of them speaks. The room is pitch dark, and they breathe in unison. On her thigh his right hand rests lightly. His fingers are cool and not quite still. He keeps the nails on his right hand long for playing the guitar. It used to excite her to see that hand on her breast, the thumb and forefinger plucking her nipple into hardness.

She has brought her own hand to her breast. She doesn't fully realize it until she feels his fingers brushing her knuckles. Something just clears out of her mind, gives up. She turns over and kisses him on the mouth.

He jerks his head back.

"It's all right," she says, meaning that everything is. Meaning that her love is panoramic, racing like an ignited wick from the night of the wedding to this moment. She kisses him again. She pushes her tongue between his teeth. She licks his teeth, bites his bottom lip. She drops onto her back and pulls him on top of her.

She keep clinging to him as he sits up. She thinks he's trying to get away. But he kneels between her legs and parts her labia with his fingers. Then he licks her there. It's the first time this has been done to her. She assumes it's preliminary. He keeps it up, though, soft, steady, devoted, cat-like licking until her body begins to loosen. Her joints unhinge. Her vulva breaks free and levitates, and her skin spreads like dough, a lovely, funny sensation, and then a disturbing one. And then she doesn't care—she'd die to prolong it.

Her orgasm is like a series of electric shocks. Her pelvis jolts and her vagina contracts almost painfully. "I love you," Sam says urgently, as if he knows that she's in new territory. "I love you, I love you," over and over until she lies still.

"Oh, my God," she says then. "I love *you*," she says. She hasn't told him in five months. After a moment she says, "It's you I love." Under the circumstances that sounds more precise, more to the point. Tomorrow he is going into the hospital. Flying down to Boston by himself. Since she wouldn't talk about it, wouldn't even think about it, there was never any question of her going with him. Now, for the first time, she allows herself to wonder what will happen. She is still not ready for details, but she asks if the operation is dangerous.

"Apparently not," he says. "I mean, not life-threatening."

She turns to him and places her hand over his crotch. She knows he's wearing underwear, which makes it easier.

"Don't!" he says, wrenching sideways.

"No, let me," she says and puts her hand back. She presses her palm down and feels the springiness of his pubic hair. "It's just like me," she says, oddly relieved.

He doesn't move.

"It's you," she says.

"It is," he says. "And it isn't." He takes her hand and holds it to his chest. Then he covers them both with the sheet.

He is still holding her hand when she wakes up. His head is arched back and he's snoring, a soft purring sound. It's morning. There's a band of grey light between the drapes, and another band flaring across the ceiling.

If somebody were looking down on them, Marion thinks—if, for instance, her mother's spirit was that clean, geometrical flare—they would seem like any other man and wife. They would seem content, she thinks. Peaceful, and lucky. Two people unacquainted with grief. They would seem like two happily married, perfectly normal people.